"I hurt you? If I did I'm sorry—"

"You didn't *hurt* me! At least, not in the way you think!"

The defiant tilt to her chin was pure provocation. His heart gave a sharp kick, making his blood pound heavily through his system. He wanted to hold her close, kiss away the blaze of rejection in her eyes…

"Cassandra, *querida*, you know what you do to me."

And what he did to her. And it was happening right now, no matter how hard she struggled against it.

His kiss was pure Joaquin. Pure enticement; pure seduction in a caress. It snatched her thoughts from her brain, reduced what was left to nothing but mush, and left her adrift on a sea of sensation—floating, melting, not knowing where she had been going or why.

Harlequin Presents®

The Alcolar Family

Proud, modern-day Spanish aristocrats—passion is their birthright!

Harlequin Presents® is proud to present international bestselling author Kate Walker's new ALCOLAR FAMILY miniseries.

Meet the Alcolar Family:
Joaquin: The first born and only legitimate Alcolar son. Can he forget his no-commitment rule and make his twelve-month mistress his wife?

Coming soon:
The Spaniard's Inconvenient Wife
October 2005 #2498
Ramon: The beloved illegitimate son, he gets more than he bargained for in his carefully planned marriage of convenience!

Bound by Blackmail
November 2005 #2504
Mercedes: Can the only Alcolar daughter find the man who is her match?

Kate Walker is the author of more than 40 romance novels for Harlequin Presents®. To find out about Kate, and her forthcoming books, visit her Web site at www.kate-walker.com

Kate Walker

THE TWELVE-MONTH MISTRESS

The Alcolar Family

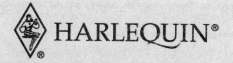

HARLEQUIN®

TORONTO • NEW YORK • LONDON
AMSTERDAM • PARIS • SYDNEY • HAMBURG
STOCKHOLM • ATHENS • TOKYO • MILAN • MADRID
PRAGUE • WARSAW • BUDAPEST • AUCKLAND

ISBN 0-373-12492-9

THE TWELVE-MONTH MISTRESS

First North American Publication 2005.

www.eHarlequin.com

Printed in U.S.A.

CHAPTER ONE

THE calendar hung in the middle of the wall, right where Cassie couldn't avoid seeing it.

No matter which way she looked, it was always there, clear and obvious. In fact it almost seemed to be getting bigger, more obvious with each second that passed, the photograph of a fiesta scene instantly attracting attention with its brilliant colours, its vibrant life.

And beneath it, the dates in bold black print.

Particularly the date she didn't want to see.

Or most longed to see. She didn't know which way she felt right now.

Because the importance of that date wasn't in her hands. It was in Joaquin's control. And only his. She could do nothing about it.

Not if she wanted to avoid pushing things in a direction she didn't want them to go.

But was it worth staying in a situation that was just not making her happy?

'Oh, stop it!' she told herself sharply, pushing back a strand of golden blonde hair that had fallen forward over her face, and tucking it behind her ear. 'Leave it! You're just going round in circles!'

As she had been doing for the last three weeks, she admitted, arching brows drawing sharply together over concerned blue eyes. Ever since the calendar had been turned to reveal the month of June and right there, in the middle of the third week, the all-important anniversary.

The anniversary that she had no idea whether Joaquin would remember and, if he did, whether he would mark it in the way that he had done with all his other previous relationships.

By leaving.

Or, rather, telling her to leave, seeing as it was his house that they lived in.

No woman had ever lasted more than twelve months with him. After a year, sometimes even to the day, he said good-bye and walked away without a backwards glance, it seemed. And at the end of this week she would have been living with him for a year.

'Oh, Joaquin, what are you thinking? What are you *feeling*?'

Would she ever be more than just a mistress to him, or was she destined to go the same way as all his other women—out of his life for good?

The sound of a key being inserted in a lock downstairs pulled her out of her thoughts and into the present moment again. Somehow she had missed the sound of the car pulling up outside and now here he was, Joaquin himself, unexpectedly early, and she would have to get herself into the right mood to greet him.

'Cassandra!

The sound of her name, pronounced as only Joaquin could speak it, with the lilting emphasis, the faint roll of the R, floated up the stairs to her waiting ears. Ears that were straining to hear whether there was anything different about the way he used it, anything that would give her a clue as to just what sort of mood he was in. Whether he was feeling as he usually did, or if some unwanted distance, a newfound coldness had crept into his tone.

Anything that might give her warning of what was to come. Anything that would give her a couple of much-needed seconds to adjust her own mood, her own response, prepare herself if necessary.

'Cassie!'

Oh, there was no mistaking *that* tone, she told herself wryly.

Even on the single word, the darker emphasis, the undercurrent of impatience was pure Joaquin. And, unlike most people who used the shortened version of her name as a form of affection and warmth, Joaquin Alcolar employed it as a sound of reproof, an indication that she had somehow fallen short of his expectations.

Obviously he had expected that she would have rushed to greet him, to kiss him, as he came through the door. On any other day she would have fulfilled those expectations with alacrity. But today her troubled thoughts had made her unusually slow to react.

'Cassie! Where are you?'

'Up here!'

She was moving as she spoke. There had been a note in his voice that had her up and out of her chair before she even had time to think. A note that went beyond his usual, ingrained belief that he had only to speak and he would be obeyed.

He was right, of course. As the eldest son of Juan Ramón Alcolar, the Spanish aristocrat who also owned and ran the Alcolar Corporation, Joaquin had been used to respect and obedience to his command, the fulfilment of every whim, from the day of his birth. And now, as owner and managing director of his own highly successful vineyard, he had increased both his status and his personal fortune two-hundredfold, so demanding even more respect than ever before.

That was why some called him *El Lobo*, lone wolf, because he had gone his own way in the world, looking to no one for help, not even his family. But there were others who changed one letter of the nickname, making it into *El Loco*, because they just couldn't believe that anyone would turn their back on the fortune and the position his father would have given him if he had gone into the family media business instead.

'I'm coming!'

She wasn't always so swift to obey him. In the past she had sometimes held out against that note of command in his voice, deliberately defying him just to rile his volatile temper. And she was one of the few, along with his younger sister Mercedes, who could get away with it.

Normally she was more than happy to provoke him if she felt he needed it, determinedly rebelling against that autocratic assumption that he had only to speak to be obeyed. But not today. Not now. Not with that all-important anniversary coming up fast and Joaquin's mood so uncertain.

'You're early! I wasn't expecting you for an hour or more.'

And she didn't sound too pleased about it, Joaquin reflected inwardly, knowing that this was one of the reasons that had brought him home so unexpectedly. Cassandra had changed recently. Changed in ways he didn't understand or like, and he'd hoped that by catching her unawares he might have a chance at finding out just what was going on in her mind.

'The meeting reached the decision I wanted far sooner than I had anticipated. And I have plenty of work to do on the next project so I decided to take advantage of the fact and come home.'

His concentration had been shot anyway. His mind hadn't been on the matter in hand and so he'd brought the meeting to an abrupt halt and headed out to his car as soon as he could. He suspected he'd broken a couple of speed limits on his way back too.

'Why does that surprise you? Do you have a guilty conscience about something?'

'What? No. Of course not.'

It sounded disturbingly edgy. Her voice rose and fell in

an unnatural way, making her sound as if she had something to hide.

'It's just that you said you wouldn't be back until seven.'

'Because I didn't expect to be. I also didn't think that you'd complain.'

'I'm not complaining.'

She'd been like this for a couple of weeks now, growing sharper and more unpredictable with each day that passed. And nothing made her smile as she had once smiled so readily. Nothing pleased her.

That was, nothing but their time in bed. That at least hadn't lost its appeal. If anything, his appetite seemed to have grown stronger, more passionate—though there was less of the true lover in Cassandra. A lot less of the seductive, enticing lover, and much more of an urgent demand that shook him with its intensity.

Something had gone out of their relationship and left it all the poorer for its absence.

'I'm not complaining—it's just unexpected.'

She had reached the top of the stairs now, looking down at where he stood at the bottom, feet planted firmly on the terracotta tiles of the hall floor, dark head tilted back so that he could look up at her.

Even from this perspective, a position that would have foreshortened and distorted a lesser man, he was imposing and forcefully stunning in a way that rocked her already precarious composure, notching her heartbeat up a pace, making her blood throb in her veins.

Hair as black as a raven's wing, worn slightly long at the neck, matched exactly the jet darkness of his eyes. His skin was deep olive satin, tanned even more by the burning sun in this part of Jerez. He was unusually tall for a Spaniard, his height revealing his Andalusian ancestry, and the broad chest, narrow waist and long, powerful legs of his strong, lean body were sensuously enhanced by the superb tailoring of his pale grey suit, the white shirt underneath worn with a silvery silk tie.

The tie he had tugged loose at the throat, of course. Joaquin Alcolar might be accustomed to wearing the conventional uniform of the successful businessman when he had to, but as soon as he got home he would abandon the sophisticated veneer. He'd discard the tailored jacket, unfasten the tie and the top couple of buttons of his shirt, and transform himself from the powerful managing director into something much less formal and constrained, appearing so much more rakish, more potently virile.

'When the meeting finished early I decided that I could get more done at home than I could in the office.'

'You've come home to *work*, then?'

It shouldn't hurt. She knew what he was like. But it did sting smartly just the same.

'I would have thought you'd be pleased.'

'I am.'

She sounded as if she had forced herself to say it, Joaquin reflected, the uneasy, irritated mood in which he had arrived home growing by the second. And what was she doing hovering up there at the top of the stairs when she should be coming down here, into his arms?

That was what he wanted. But just lately what he wanted and what Cassandra wanted had been totally separate things. The warm spontaneity that had taken him so much by storm had vanished, leaving in its place a cool constraint that jarred unpleasantly.

'If this is pleased, then I don't think I'd like to see you disappointed. You look almost as if you have something to hide. What is it, *querida*? Do you have a lover hidden away upstairs? Someone you don't want me to see?'

He meant it to be light, joking, but his inner feelings added a darker edge that made it seem more like an attack than he had intended.

'Oh, don't be ridiculous!'

She was on the step just above him now, looking down into his eyes, and he saw the faintest flicker of something in their depths that made his hackles rise as her blue gaze clashed with his much darker one.

'Why would I want a lover?'

'Why indeed? Don't I keep you busy enough?'

This was her cue to move into his arms, to press the softness of her cheek against the dark-shadowed skin of his, and to wind her own arms around him as she snuggled close.

To distract him from the uneasy, uncomfortable path his thoughts had been following for far too long now.

'Cassandra?'

There it was again, that sudden unexplained smokiness in the normally brilliant blue eyes, making him want to grab at her arms, shake them, shake *her* into saying what was wrong. If anything was wrong. Because he was sure there was something.

'Of course you do.'

Her smile was a disturbing on-off flash, withdrawn and meaningless, no real warmth in it at all.

'More than busy.'

And at last she bent and kissed him. But it was only the brush of her lips against his cheek. There and then gone— as elusive as her mood had been so often recently.

And there was that damn smile again. A smile that was not a smile. A smile that said that her thoughts were some- where else entirely. Not with him at all.

He hated the way that made him feel.

The next minute she had come down the final step, gently pushing past him as she moved into the hall, turning towards the kitchen.

'I was going to make coffee. Do you want some? Or perhaps something cool. It was terribly hot when I was outside this afternoon.'

'It's no cooler now.'

What the hell were they doing talking about the *weather*? He used inane conversations about the climate to while away time with people he didn't know or like. People he couldn't get on with. Business contacts, employees—his father!

Not his mistress—the woman he lived with!

'So not coffee, then?'

'No!'

It was not the offer of coffee or any other drink he was referring to. He couldn't stand the way that she was walking away from him. Not looking at him. Not even addressing him face on, but tossing the remarks back over her shoulder as if she didn't care whether he heard her or not.

'No!'

He moved after her, anger charging his strides, making them long, swift, furious. His hand came out, clamped over her upper arm, jolting her to a halt, whirling her round.

'Joaquin!'

But he ignored her protest; heedless of whether he had caused it by the way his hard fingers were digging into the white flesh exposed by the sleeveless turquoise sundress. Burning dark eyes searched her face once more, wanting to probe deep into her mind, her soul, see what was hidden there.

'No!' he said again, though even he couldn't have said with regard to what. He only knew that he didn't like the way he was feeling. The way he had been feeling for too long.

The way she made him feel.

And the way he had never, ever felt in his life before.

He wanted his old way of life back. Wanted that feeling of being in control, of knowing where he was heading— what he wanted! He hated this sensation of being adrift in a rudderless boat—and all because of this woman.

'All right, no coffee. Just what is the matter with you today?'

But he wasn't ready to answer that.

'Nothing. Nothing's the matter.'

'Then stop behaving like a bear with a sore head. I want a drink even if you don't, so...'

Her gaze dropped to the strong, tanned fingers still clenched around her arm, then back up to his face, the reproach in them so strong that he instinctively released her, taking a step back.

'*Perdón.*'

'Okay.'

She flashed that meaningless smile once again. *Dios*, but he truly hated the insincerity of it! But then almost immediately her expression changed.

'No, actually, it's not okay! Not at all! There's nothing okay about it. What do you think you're doing—manhandling me like that?'

'Manhandling?'

In his indignation, his accent and pronunciation mangled the word so that it was almost incomprehensible.

'*Manhandling?* You call that manhandling? What has happened to you, my Cassie? You never used to be like this. You always used to like my touch...'

A rush of cold anger at her rejection, the words she had used, pushed him forward, eyes fixed on her face, noting the suddenly watchful expression, the flicker of something new and uncertain deep in those blue eyes.

'Loved it...'

'Well not the way you got hold of me just then! I didn't like that! And I certainly didn't *love* it!'

'I hurt you? If I did I'm sorry—'

'You didn't *hurt* me! At least, not in the way you think!'

The defiant tilt to her chin was pure provocation; an extra spark in the brilliance of her eyes created an answering fire in the most primitively masculine parts of his body. His heart gave a sharp kick, making his blood pound heavily through his system.

And suddenly he knew that he had to touch her. Really touch her. And not in the way that she had accused him of, *manhandling* her. He wanted to hold her close, kiss away the blaze of rejection in her eyes…

'And you can *perdón* till you're blue in the face and it won't do a blind bit of good!' she flung at him furiously. 'You're not going to treat me like this and get away with it!'

The sting of the words made him check himself. Think. He didn't like the direction his thoughts led him in.

Joaquin drew his brows together sharply, not knowing in the mixture of disbelief, incomprehension and anger that was suddenly bubbling inside him exactly which emotion was uppermost. His frown revealed them all.

'Treat you in what way, precisely, *querida*? Cassandra, you're really not making sense. And just what brought on this mood in the first place?'

'You did!'

She was treading on dangerous ground here, Cassie admitted to herself. If she wasn't prepared to tell him the real truth, then she was taking a risk even hinting at it. She had vowed that until Joaquin himself raised the topic of their year together then she wouldn't say a word. Wouldn't even hint at the way it was making her feel.

But an accusation like that last one came too close to what was really tearing her up inside.

'And you can keep your hands off me!'

'Oh, no, my lovely…'

He shook his dark head slowly but so emphatically, his voice a predatory purr.

'That I cannot do. It is impossible. I cannot be with you, near you, and not touch you. I only have to look at you to want you, and you know that. Even now, when you are in this wild, crazy mood, my fingers itch to touch…'

He suited action to the words, reaching out and hooking one hand very gently around the back of her neck, the warmth of his palm along the soft skin of her throat, his thumb brushing her cheek.

'To caress you.'

That strong, broad thumb moved against her flesh, stroking delicate, erotic circles that woke every nerve, bringing their endings rushing to the surface.

'To hold you.'

His other hand trailed softly up the right side of her neck, silky touch moving over satin and raising cold prickles of awareness all over her body as it did so, making her shiver in uncontrollable response. A moment later her face was cupped in both his hands, being drawn slowly and irresistibly towards him.

'Kiss you...' he murmured, his breath warm against her lips.

No! It was a cry of protest in her mind as panic set in at the thought of just how easily he could do this. How casually, how often he used the fierce, blazing, physical passion between them to avoid anything truly emotional. To dodge talking about anything that mattered.

Like their future. If they had one.

She tried to shake her head, to break away, but he held her too firmly for that.

'Cassandra, *querida*, you know what you do to me.'

And what he did to her. And it was happening right now, no matter how hard she struggled against it.

His kiss was pure Joaquin. Pure enticement; pure seduction in a caress. It snatched her thoughts from her brain, reduced what was left to nothing but mush, and left her adrift on a sea of sensation, floating, melting, not knowing where she had been going or why.

'Joaquin...'

His name was a sigh against his mouth, drawn from her by the pressure of his lips on hers.

'So now, *mi belleza*, how am I doing now?'

She could hear the smile in his voice though she couldn't actually see it on his face.

'How am I touching you?'

Warm arms slid round her, closing tight across her shoulders, drawing her to him with soft but irresistible strength.

'How am I holding you? Am I *manhandling* you now?'

'N-No...'

'Should I take my hands off you?'

'No!'

It was a cry of protest when the pressure of his arms eased slightly, and it seemed he would have drawn away.

'No—not now...'

In her heart, even that faint lessening of his hold felt like a little death, like the loss of something most precious to her, and something she would do all she could to keep.

But at the same time, unwanted and unwelcome, a tiny, lingering voice of common sense was whispering at the back of what was left of her mind, underneath all the sensual onslaught.

No, no, no, no...it was saying, over and over. And in a very different tone from the one she had used.

It was like being in the middle of an emotional civil war where one part of her yearned to surrender to the sexual appeal of Joaquin's touch, the heat that his kiss triggered all through her body. But at the same time that warning voice was demanding to know why she was making this so easy for him. Why she was going under without a struggle.

Because she didn't want to fight. She didn't want to struggle against her own feelings, her own desire to meet his kiss with her kiss, his caress with her own gentle touch. Even after just that one kiss, the feel of his arms around her, her whole body ached with a need that she could hardly control. She yearned to crush herself closer to him, to feel the heat and masculine power of his body against her own.

'Not now...' Joaquin echoed.

His mouth was on her throat now, making a slow, seductive journey from her shoulder to her jaw, kissing his way along. And Cassie would never have thought that there could be such variety in the simple sensation of a kiss.

But now it seemed that a kiss could be both hard and soft, light and then forceful against her neck. It could be oh, so tender and enticing, so that she felt she would almost weep at the gentleness of it. And then again it could be sharply, faintly cruel when his teeth grazed her skin, occasionally nipping lightly so that she gasped in shock.

'Not now,' he repeated, the words forming against her jaw-line in the warmth of his breath. 'Now I am not man-handling you, but treating you as a woman should be treated. As a man should touch his woman—as I want to touch my woman.'

My woman.

The words were like a slap in the face, forcing her out of the heated daze into which she had fallen and making her look reality right in the eye.

My woman.

The darkly possessive tone revealed more of Joaquin than anything else could.

'So, *mi belleza*, perhaps we should continue this somewhere more comfortable, hmm?'

Mi belleza. My woman.

Always, to Joaquin, it was what he owned, what he controlled, what he had power over that mattered. He ran his life with a ruthless, almost brutal discipline. Everything was as he wanted it and nothing happened without his approval.

It was what had brought him his success and what kept him right where he was. Always at the top of his game, always on the peak of the mountain.

Always having things on his own terms, and only his terms.

She had come into his life on his terms, lived with him on his terms. And would she be expected to leave on his terms too? To walk out the door when he said it was time, whether she wanted to or not?

Was she only ever going to let him dictate things to her?

'*Querida?*'

Joaquin had noticed her sudden silence, the withdrawal that had taken her away from him, mentally if not physically.

'What is it?'

Cassie opened her mouth to reply, found that her throat was too dry and tight to form any words, and had to clear it harshly before she could manage to speak.

'I thought you came home to work. And I really need that coffee.'

At least her voice was croaky and raw enough to make it believable. She sounded as if she had a ton of sand roughening her throat and she had to lick at her lips nervously to stop them from drying out. The way his eyes followed the betraying movement had a hawklike intensity that made her shiver deep inside.

'I'm parched.'

His stillness betrayed the way he was feeling, the anger he was holding in check. Joaquin Alcolar wasn't a man who gave in to rages and blazing tempers. The fury he felt was cold, hard as ice, bitter as a cruel winter wind, but it was no less savage for that.

And it was always preceded by one of these sudden silences. The freezing of his long frame into the total stillness of a hunting predator who had spotted his prey and had every muscle tense and bunched, waiting for just the right moment to pounce.

'You're *thirsty*?'

His tone made it plain how ridiculous he thought it. How impossible it seemed to him that anyone could want to choose the simple practical need for a drink over the sensual banquet he had obviously intended enjoying.

'Yes.'

It was all she could manage. That and the brief, uncomfortable ducking of her head, carefully avoiding his burning gaze. If she looked into his eyes she would see the anger there that wasn't in his voice and she knew it would destroy her nerve to go on.

'I said I was thirsty when I came down. I'm still thirsty now. I was on my way to make a coffee...'

'You're joking, *si*?'

He couldn't believe it, she realised uncomfortably. He really couldn't believe that she would reject his seductive advances. That she would turn them down—turn *him* down.

And even worse, he hadn't ever thought that she could resist him. He had assumed that she would be putty in his hands, easily distracted from her purpose by what he wanted. That she would do as he wished, without any questions. That she would respond to his whim as swiftly and obediently as a trained dog. And that if he told her to jump then she would simply ask how high.

'Why should I be joking?'

She tried to assume an airy carelessness that she was very far from feeling. The look in those deep-set eyes was dangerous, and the strong body was still too taut, too unmoving for comfort.

'Cassie...'

Whatever he had been about to say, he didn't finish. Even as he spoke her name in that harsh way of his, the edge on the word so rough that it scraped its way over her exposed skin, there was the sound of another key being inserted into the lock behind them.

A moment later the door was pushed open, swinging back on its hinges until it slammed against the wall with an ominous-sounding thud. A man, tall, dark, strong like Joaquin, stood in the doorway framed against the still-burning sunlight outside.

'Cassie?'

Her name was spoken in a voice so very similar to

Joaquin's, the intonation, the accent an almost exact match
for his. But where Joaquin's tone had been so cold and
distant, the warmth and welcome in this one were so evident that she turned to him in instinctive relief, her eyes
lighting up, her mouth curving into a ready smile.

'Ramón! Come in!'

'Ramón.'

Joaquin's echoing of his half-brother's name held none
of the warmth and welcome that Cassie had shown.

'What are you doing here? And where the hell did you
get the keys to the house?'

'I was invited,' Ramón returned casually. 'And keys—
well, Cassie lent hers to me so that I didn't have to hang
about outside. Here, *querida*…'

He tossed the keys and a smile in Cassie's direction and
as she caught the clinking bundle she saw the brooding look
in Joaquin's dark eyes and was unable to suppress a faint
smile herself.

So Joaquin was none too pleased with his brother's sudden appearance. Perhaps even a little jealous?

Surely that was a hopeful sign? Perhaps even something
she could play on to find out the real state of her lover's
feelings?

Taking a couple of quick steps forward, she enfolded
Ramón in a warm hug, pressing her cheek to the lean, hard
planes of his.

'Come in, Ramón. Would you like a drink? We were
just about to have coffee.'

And the look on Joaquin's face as she led the way down
the hall towards the kitchen gave her a sudden lift to her
spirits that made it almost worth the risks she had taken by
provoking him in this way.

CHAPTER TWO

Damn Ramón!

'Damn, damn, damn him!'

Joaquin slammed his fist hard against the side of the window frame as he stared across at the terraced expanse of his garden, to where the clear water of the curved swimming pool glinted in the last of the afternoon sun.

Damn him for appearing at just the wrong moment! For walking into the house as if he owned it, flashing that smile at Cassandra and interrupting...

Interrupting what?

The question froze him suddenly, hand still clenched tight into a brutal fist, the knuckles of his fingers showing through white under his tanned skin.

This time, the muttered curses in his native Spanish were harsher, more savage—and aimed at himself instead of his brother and his ill-timed visit.

Interrupting what? That was the real problem. The uncomfortable, nagging worry at the bottom of his mind, that corrupted and distorted everything until he wasn't sure what to think.

He had thought that he'd succeeded in what he'd planned for his early arrival at the *finca*. That he'd enticed Cassandra out of her difficult mood, charmed away the uncharacteristic coolness and distance in her attitude—seduced it out of her. And he had believed that she was ready, as she had always been in the past, to put their differences behind them, and do their making up where they always did it so well—in bed.

But Ramón's arrival had interrupted all that. Broken the mood totally and left him fuming with frustration while his woman and his half-brother made coffee and chatted affably.

It seemed that Ramón had a habit of turning up unexpectedly, just when he was least wanted. After all, hadn't he arrived on their father's doorstep, unannounced, nothing known of him until then, just at the moment when Juan Alcolar and his son by marriage had been at the lowest point of their relationship together? And now here was Ramón, the illegitimate son—*one* of the illegitimate sons, Joaquin corrected, because there was Alex too. But Ramón was the son who was everything that his father would have wanted—who had everything going for him—except that he was not Juan's legitimate heir.

'No!'

He muttered it aloud to emphasise the word, driving it home to himself.

It wasn't Ramón's fault that he was who he was. Not Ramón's fault that their father was a philandering womaniser who couldn't keep his trousers on when he was with another female. He was their father's son after all; no one could have any doubt about that. You only had to look at the three of them together and it was as plain as could be.

And it wasn't Ramón's fault that he had wandered in on the awkward, uncomfortable confrontation between his brother and Cassandra.

The sort of awkward, uncomfortable, uneasy confrontation that was becoming more and more common between them. So much so that the nagging unease was the norm rather than the rare occurrence it had been at the beginning of their relationship.

At the beginning…

Joaquin's hard features softened from the taut, harsh lines into which they had been drawn, and a smile of memory played over his sensual mouth.

At the beginning— Oh, their relationship had been amazing then. Amazing, fantastic—mind-blowingly sensual.

They had been caught up in a whirlwind of sexual desire and passion, unable to keep their hands off each other, not daring even to kiss in public for fear of the blazing, hungry desire such a small caress might spark off. If they had been in the house, then they had been in bed. It seemed that they had never left the bedroom, except occasionally to eat, for almost all of the first six months.

But that had changed so much lately.

The frown was back, creasing his forehead harshly.

The sex was still great—the best, for him at least. Cassandra turned him on as no other woman had done in his life before. But out of bed, so often he had the uneasy feeling that her mind was somewhere else. And…

But at that moment his thoughts stopped dead, his rational process arrested by the sight beyond the window.

'Cassandra!'

Where he had opted for a shower to wash away the heat of the day and freshen up, Cassie had decided to go for a swim. So now he stood transfixed, his ebony gaze caught and held by the tall, slender figure making her way down the path towards the cool, inviting water of the pool. Her long blonde hair was caught up in a high pony-tail at the back of her head, and she wore a hot pink bikini, fastened at the back and the sides by shoestring laces.

'Bella!'

It was a fervent, almost reverent exclamation, expelled on a low, sighing breath. He had thought that after their twelve months together the effect her beauty had on him might have lessened, not hitting home quite so hard. But now he found himself caught and held unmoving by just the sight of her, and the sensation deep in the pit of his stomach felt as if someone had just punched him there, very hard.

The hot pink bikini might not be as microscopic as some things he had seen her wear in the privacy of their bedroom, but to a man who knew her body intimately the way that the tight Lycra clung to the smooth curves of her breasts and hips, even before it was wet, was pure torment. The brilliant colour of the material was in sharp contrast to the smoothness of her slender limbs, only just touched with the faintest hint of a pale gold tan after her year here.

Joaquin's mouth dried, his lower body tightening sharply at just the thought of sliding his hands over the heated satin of her flesh, over the long, lean lines of her legs, trailing along the waistband of the bottom half of the swimming costume. His touch would follow the indentation of her waist, skim over the delicate ribcage, and up, towards the soft swell of her swaying breasts.

'Hell-fire!'

This time the kick of need was sharper than before, making his head swim, his breath catch. He was hard already. Hard and hot and hungry. So much so that watching Cassie move to the edge of the pool and lift her arms above her head, bringing those luscious breasts into even sharper prominence, was like some form of delicious torment, one he wanted desperately to end and yet also longed to prolong as much as he possibly could.

He wanted this woman. Wanted her with a need that was more than words could describe. With a hunger that all the many, many times they had made love over the past twelve months could do nothing to assuage. If anything, he wanted her more now than that day when he had first set eyes on her and felt that he might die if he didn't get her into his bed—and fast!

But then she lifted herself on her toes, gave a little spring and dived neatly into the pool, disappearing under the cool water in a couple of seconds.

And before those seconds had ended, before she had a chance to fully submerge herself, Joaquin found that he was moving. The towel he had been drying his hair on was discarded somewhere, he didn't give a damn where, and he was thundering down the stairs, leaping the last section all in one jump, and dashing out, on bare feet, towards the terrace and the pool.

Her blonde head had barely just broken the surface as he arrived at the spot from which she had dived, the golden hair sleeked and darkened by the water, the long pony-tail floating on the surface beside her. And as he checked briefly at the edge of the pool she shook the water from her face, kicked her legs and set out at a steady breaststroke for the far side, away from him.

She hadn't seen him, didn't know that he was there. But she would do soon. He had no intention of hanging around here, waiting. He wanted her in his arms, her body tight against his. And he wanted that *now*.

Barely pausing for breath, he executed a perfect racing dive, plunging into the water and setting off after her in a fast, powerful crawl.

The first indication Cassie had of Joaquin's presence in the pool was the sudden splash, the sound of his powerful body entering the water in a clean dive. The next moment he had surfaced and was coming after her, strong arms cleaving through the waves he'd created in forceful strokes.

A shattering range of feelings assailed her, whirling through her mind in quick succession, battering her with swift, violent changes of mood.

Shock was first. Simple, startled, physical shock at the unexpectedness of his arrival, the suddenness of the splash and swirling waves at his appearance.

Apprehension followed. Uncertainty at not knowing why he was here, what he wanted, just what his mood might be this time.

But then, suddenly, old habits reasserted themselves. Old habits of thought and actions as she recalled the number of times in the past that he had come after her in just this way. Knowing she was a strong swimmer, he had thrown out an unspoken challenge, encouraging her to race him to the far end of the pool.

'Okay, then…'

Reacting instinctively she turned, ducked under the water, kicked hard and, surfacing fast, struck out for the blue-painted edge.

At first she had a noticeable lead, but a quick glance over her shoulder showed that Joaquin was coming up fast behind her. Exhilaration and excitement flooded her veins, pushing her into even stronger movement, putting all her heart and energy into it.

She was holding her own. The finishing line was almost within reach. But Joaquin's tanned arms, his dark head, were drawing level, matching her stroke for stroke.

She saw him turn his head. Caught the swift, brilliant flash of white teeth against the dark olive of his skin as he grinned in wicked triumph. Another forceful kick from his muscular legs, an extra spurt of speed, and he had passed her, tanned fingers reaching out and touching the edge of the pool just bare seconds before her own paler ones.

'Okay, you win!'

Somehow all the uneasiness of earlier that afternoon had evaporated, leaving her with a rush along with her gasps for air as she regained her breath. Letting her feet sink slowly to the base of the pool, she stood upright in the shallower water, wiping her hands across her skin and back over her hair in order to brush away the lingering water, clearing it from her face and her eyes.

Joaquin lounged just feet away, half in, half out of the water, his back against the tiled edge of the pool, his hair, jet-black and slicked back, clinging to the fine shape of his skull. Once more those white teeth flashed in a wicked, triumphant grin.

'Show-off!'

But of course he had every right to show off, she admitted inwardly. Unlike herself, he was hardly even breathing faster; the broad, muscled chest rose and fell as easily as if he had just had a short, casual stroll along the side of the pool and not powerhoused his way through the water after her.

Glinting in the sunlight, tiny drops of water slid over the bronzed skin and came together in a tiny rivulet that trailed its way through the black body hair and down over the flat plane of his stomach. Cassie found that her mouth had dried suddenly, her throat tightening on a wave of response, and she tried to swallow as inconspicuously as possible in order to ease the constricting sensation.

Joaquin treated her to another wide grin, eyes gleaming knowingly.·

'Maybe, but I still won! So now you owe me.'

Something tightened deep in Cassie's stomach, twisting sharply on a touch of nerves.

It was no good trying to pretend that she didn't know what he meant. From the very first time when he had discovered how much she liked to swim, and how fast she was in the water, he had issued a challenge, tempting her to race him.

'And to make it interesting,' he'd said, 'we'll compete for a prize. Whoever loses owes the winner a forfeit—whatever they demand.'

So now, seeing that taunting smile, hearing the words 'you owe me,' Cassie knew just what was going through his mind.

'It wasn't a proper challenge!' she hedged warily.

'Which it wasn't the last time—when you won,' Joaquin reminded her. 'But as I recall you still claimed your prize.'

That gleam in his eyes brightened vividly, reminding her without words just what the prize she'd claimed had been, and letting her know that he remembered only too well. She felt as if her whole body must be blushing, her skin suffused with rich colour as she recalled the passionate way he had responded to her begging him to make love to her right here, in the pool, under cover of the darkness of late evening.

But that had been over a month ago. It was five weeks since they'd last raced in this way. Five weeks since they had even swum together. Five weeks in which Joaquin had had little time for relaxation, little time for leisure, little time, it seemed, for *her*. So that now things seemed so very different. The unspoken split that had opened between them had turned into a gap and from a gap into a chasm, until she was beginning to wonder if it was possible to bridge it at all.

And the worst thing was that she knew she was partly responsible. That her own inability to hide her feelings, her constrained, preoccupied mood, had driven a wedge between them and she hadn't been able to stop it.

This time she did slick her tongue over her painfully dry lips. She just couldn't stop herself.

'So what is it that you want?'

Watching that gleam flare into flame, blazing suddenly in the darkness of his gaze, she knew just what was in his mind. But a second later, to her bewilderment, he closed down on the heat in his eyes, and instead let his stare fall to her mouth.

'A kiss,' he said softly. 'Just a kiss. Is that too much to ask?'

But would it stop at just a kiss? She doubted it.

A kiss that would lead to an open mouth? A kiss that would lead to a caress, the smoothing, stroking of his hands all over her body? A kiss that would lead to lovemaking?

Was that what she wanted?

But did she care?

There was no room inside her head for the memory of the uncertainty of earlier that day. And other thoughts were crowding into her mind, making it spin even more wildly.

The exhilaration sparked by the race was still fizzing through her veins, buzzing inside her head so that she couldn't think clearly. The sheer sensual pleasure of standing here, with the sun warm on her head and shoulders, the cool water lapping around her waist, was enough to make her forget any colder, calmer, common sense. And there were other feelings too. Feelings sparked by the sight of Joaquin's lean brown body, the tight lines of his muscles still glistening with traces of moisture. The stunningly carved face was turned towards her, gilded by the sun, black eyes brilliant as jet, the high, slanting cheekbones sharp as blades under the bronze skin.

She felt dizzy with excitement, tension, admiration.

Need surfaced, caught and held.

And need she gave into, reaching out a hand that shook faintly to smooth it over the broad, straight lines of his shoulders, the strength of his arms and then along the ridges of muscle that lined his powerful chest, tracing tiny, erotic circles in the dark body hair that hazed his flesh.

'Cassandra...'

Joaquin stirred convulsively under her touch, his voice husky and soft.

'So do I get my kiss?'

Like someone in a trance she leaned forward, pressed her lips softly against the hard plane of his lean cheek, feeling the faint roughness of male skin beneath her mouth, tasting the intensely personal flavour of him. On a sigh she inhaled the equally intimate scent of his body.

And knew that she was lost.

And that she didn't give a damn.

'That, *querida*,' Joaquin complained as she withdrew slightly, 'was not a kiss. It does not pay the forfeit you owe me.'

With an effort Cassie forced herself to look up, into the sensually darkened pools of his eyes, knowing from his smile that he saw his answer in her own gaze.

'Oh, doesn't it?' she managed huskily. 'Then I shall have to do better.'

'Much better.'

'Then what about this?'

She had barely finished speaking before she took his mouth, teasing and tantalising him with her own lips, letting her tongue run along the warm cleft that separated the finely carved upper lip from the fuller, more sensual lower one. And she knew his reaction when she heard him catch in a breath on a faint gasp, his mouth opening under hers, his tongue meeting the tentative exploration with an erotic enticement, drawing her in deeper and closer.

'That's more like it,' he muttered, rough and urgent against her mouth. '*That* is a kiss. The sort of kiss I wanted.'

And as his kiss encouraged her, so his arms drew her closer too, fastening tight around her slim waist and pulling her sharply towards him. So sharply that her feet left the bottom of the pool and she floated towards him on the gentle eddies of the cool water.

But there was nothing gentle, or cool, about the part of his body that she connected with as she came tight up against him, her stomach cradled in the hard arc of his pelvis, her hips crushed against his.

And what she felt was hard and hot and intensely male. The forceful power of his arousal, reaching through the thin and ineffective barrier of her clinging costume, sent a shudder of response rushing through her. And that tiny movement only added to the stunned sense of intimacy as she was crushed closer.

'Señor Alcolar!' she managed on a choking gasp, turning shock into a teasing provocation. 'You—you have no clothes on!'

Joaquin's grin in response was totally unrepentant.

'Nothing at all,' he returned smoothly, lowering his dark head to press a hot, hungry kiss on her shoulder, one that stirred the potent heat of his lower body, pressing even more intimately against her.

Joaquin adjusted his position, opening his legs so that she was drawn into the space between them, then closing them again around her, imprisoning her tightly, his hands on her hips, warm fingers brushing against her skin.

'You're naked. And—and *aroused*...'

'Absolutely,' he nodded smilingly. 'But then...'

His grin widened, there was a faint tug between her legs, and the next moment he raised his hand from under the water to reveal the bright pink material of the bottom half of her bikini crushed in his large male hand.

'So are you.'

While his eyes had held hers, keeping her attention transfixed, his fingers had been busy under water, pulling loose the bow-tied strings that had fastened her bikini bottom over both hips, and sliding it away from her body.

Now he tossed the sliver of cerise material from him, aiming it back over his shoulder so that it landed on the bright blue tiles that surrounded the pool.

'Joaquin!'

Cassie didn't know if her startled response was one of reproof or delight, and clearly Joaquin didn't care as he settled her into an ever more intimate position between his powerful thighs, the thrust of his manhood hard against her, and brought his mouth down crushingly on hers.

And while he kept her mouth from speaking, effectively stopping her thoughts from functioning too, once more those wicked hands were busy, twitching loose the ties on her bikini top and letting it fall free, floating on the top of the clear water.

'So now you too are naked.' He spoke huskily, looking deep into her eyes, resting his forehead against hers. 'Naked and—*aroused*?'

He echoed her own words, adding an upward, questioning note at the end of the sentence, but Cassie had no doubt that he knew exactly how she was feeling.

He must know it from the way that her pulse was thudding, her heightened breathing and the vein at the base of her throat giving away too much. And the pressure of his hands at her hips was lighter than her own instinctive movement towards him, the way that she was writhing softly against his heat and hardness, revelling in the extra sensation since he had tossed aside her clothing.

And when his hands, cool and wet, came up out of the water to cup her breasts, softly teasing their peaking nipples, she knew it was impossible to hide her need from him. She didn't even want to try.

'What do you think?'

She whispered it against his ear, her head lifted to press against his cheek, and she let her teeth graze the skin of his earlobe very slightly, feeling the long body crushed against hers shudder in instant response.

'I think…'

Those knowing hands were on the move again, wandering over her body, stroking the swaying curves of her breasts.

'I think it might be so. But I also think…'

His fingers slid down under water, travelling over the flat plane of her stomach, smoothed through the wet curls at the juncture of her thighs, slid lower…

'Joaquin!' Cassie gasped as his daringly intimate touch made her insides clench, her whole body convulsing on a wave of hungry need. 'Oh, please…'

'I think that you should say—that you should tell me how you feel—don't you?' he urged softly, a knowing smile curving up the corners of his wickedly sensual mouth in the same moment that his deep, deep eyes took in the unconcealed evidence of the effect his touch was having on her.

'Joaquin…' she moaned as a searching finger slid into the moist cleft, found the tiny, pulsing bud and touched softly, creating an effect much like setting light to the fuse on a powder keg.

'*Tell* me…' he persisted, almost roughly, clearly determined that she should say exactly what she wanted even though it had to be so blatantly obvious that it was impossible he didn't know. 'Cassandra, *querida*, tell me.'

'I think—I *know*—I want you! *Want* you!'

And now that she'd said the words, she couldn't hold them back, but repeated them over and over in a growing litany of need.

'I want you, want you,' she muttered with her mouth against his shoulder, her teeth scraping his tanned skin, her fingers digging into the tight muscles.

She heard his muttered curse, felt the struggle he was having to contain himself, control himself, and was determined to break it down totally, absolutely.

'Want you here with me, close to me, inside me... Joaquin, I need you!'

'And I want you!'

It was a cry of surrender, an admission of total loss of control. His eyes were wild and blazing, his face set in a mask of urgent need as he stood up, hands closing over her, swinging her up into his arms and hoisting her bodily out of the pool and up the shallow steps, trailing dripping water behind them as he carried her over to one of the wooden loungers and set her down, not exactly gently, on the green-and-white striped cushions.

'Now...'

This was what he wanted, Joaquin told himself as he looked down at Cassie, sprawled on the lounger, her wet blonde hair struggling loose from the pony-tail in which it had been fastened.

This woman, hot and hungry and wild—this was what he wanted from the relationship. This was what was worth having, worth putting up with any other uncomfortable feelings for. This burned away the unease, the doubt, leaving room for only one, blazingly powerful emotion.

Lowering himself to kneel at the side of the lounger, he picked up one slim, elegant foot, still damp from the swimming pool, and pressed a kiss against the big toe.

'Joaquin...' Cassie protested, but only faintly. 'We're out in the open...'

'And there isn't another house for miles,' he returned smoothly, moving on to all the other toes in succession. 'No one to see us. Besides, that didn't trouble you that other time.'

'We were in the pool then—the water—oh!'

She broke off sharply, her eyes closing, her head moving restlessly against the cushion as his warm mouth closed over one toe and his tongue circled it enticingly.

'We're as private here as in the bedroom,' Joaquin told her, abandoning her toes and turning his attention to her foot, kissing his way from her instep to her ankle. 'So just lie back and let me pleasure you.'

If the truth were told, he didn't know if he was pleasuring her or himself, he admitted inwardly as he made his slow, caressing way up her leg, heading for the softer inner skin of her thighs, one of the parts of a woman that he loved most of all. There were times when only the hot, hard rush of fiery passion would do, when speed and urgency were everything. And there were times when the slow, sensual build-up, the piling of delight upon delight, was what it was all about.

And this time was one of those.

This was a time to savour. To enjoy to the fullest the pleasures of the flesh.

But at the touch of his mouth on her thigh Cassie moaned aloud, her hands reaching down, reaching for him, pulling him up to cover her until their mouths met, clashed, clung in a soul-searing kiss that was hotter than the sun in the sky.

'*Querida!*' Joaquin muttered against her lips, the sensation of her naked, sun-warmed body under his pushing all his earlier thoughts of patience, of slow sensuality, right out of his mind. 'Cassandra, *querida*, you are all that a man could ever ask for in a woman—in a lover.'

His strong, tanned legs pushed at her slimmer, paler ones, opening her to him so that he lay between them, the essential heat and hardness of him just nudging against her exposed flesh.

'Joaquin...'

It was a soft, moaning whisper, the sound of his name an enticement, a caress and a reproof all in one.

And the reproof was because she was getting impatient. He could see it in her face, read the gathering storm of hunger in her eyes.

That was what he had always enjoyed so much about this woman.

The fact that she not only matched his desire head-on, but that her own passion often surged ahead, leaving him breathless with the need to equal her, satiate her, appease the hunger her demands woke in him.

He had never had a sexual partner like her. Never known someone who satisfied all his fantasies in one glorious, sensual, physical package, and yet somehow always managed to leave him hungry, looking for more.

Cassie's clutching hands held him where he was, close on top of her body. The soft, sweet pressure of her breasts against his chest was a torment of sensuous delight, making him harden even more.

With his lips taking delicate, nipping little caresses, he kissed his way down her neck, making her stir and murmur faintly, tilting her head back against the cushions. The movement opened the way to the rest of her upper body, taking his kisses over the slopes of her breasts, one after the other, so she arced ever higher, exposing the hardened, thrusting nipples to tempt him.

A temptation there was no way in hell he could resist.

'Oh, dear heaven...!'

The uncontrolled cry escaped her as his mouth fastened tight over the pink nub, suckling hard, grazing the skin faintly with his teeth.

'Oh, Joaquin…'

Her body convulsed under his, her legs opening wider, exposing the innermost core of her, inviting…

With a single, forceful, uncontrollable thrust, he answered that invitation, taking himself into her body and into the realms of pure sensation in the space of a split second.

There was no room for thought in his head. No room for anything but sheer physical delight. Hunger, passion, burning, blazing excitement that exploded inside his brain, took him higher, further…

And Cassandra came with him every inch of the way.

Having been together for a year, their bodies were attuned. Each knew the other's private pleasure spots, and used that knowledge shamelessly to entice, to tantalise, to arouse even further. And the warmth of the sun, playing over bare flesh, the evening scent of the plants in the garden, the sound of the birds chirping in the trees, were extra enhancements to the erotic pleasure that swamped their thoughts.

They were lost, abandoned. Totally absorbed in each other. Totally given up to each other, the primitive rhythm pulsing harder, hotter, faster, higher. Until it took them right over the edge and into the mind-blowing explosion of perfect ecstasy, falling headlong into an oblivion of delight.

As their breathing gradually slowed, Joaquin buried his face against her neck, under the now-dry, tangled fall of her hair, and kissed away the faint sheen of perspiration from her skin.

'This is why you're mine, Cassandra,' he muttered, his voice thick and rough with satisfaction. 'This is why we're together, why we've stayed together. Why we've lasted this long.'

His breath escaped in a long sigh that stirred her almost-dry hair.

'You're *mine*!' he declared possessively, making it plain that that was as much as he wanted.

And at that moment, replete and totally exhausted by the blazing, primitive ardour of their lovemaking, Cassandra allowed herself to believe that perhaps, after all, for now that might just be enough for her too.

CHAPTER THREE

THAT comforting delusion stayed with her at least through the rest of the night. The truth was that she didn't have time to think of anything else.

She had barely recovered from the whirlwind assault on her senses of Joaquin's lovemaking, her breath still coming raggedly and unevenly, the sheen of perspiration drying on her skin in the cooling sun of the evening, when he had picked her up and carried her into the house.

'Joaquin…' she tried to protest feebly, but he blithely ignored her, padding over the tiles in his bare feet as he took her through the hall and up the staircase to the bedroom.

There, he laid her carefully on the bed, coming down beside her, and drawing her close, crushing a hard, impassioned kiss onto her mouth.

And Cassie surrendered all thought of protesting further, or even of trying to talk. She simply melted into the sensual appeal of his embrace, revelling in the feel of his hot, hard body against her own flesh, the scent of his skin in her nostrils.

Tonight, she told herself, for tonight she would forget her worries, put aside her concerns. Tonight she would not think of a tomorrow or ask for a future. Tonight she would simply enjoy what Joaquin offered, and only that. And she would not ask for more.

And right now what Joaquin did offer was good enough for her. More than good enough, she thought on a swooning sense of pleasure, as, muttering a litany of praise in his native Spanish, his lyrically accented voice roughened by growing desire, he kissed his way once more down from her lips to her throat, from her throat to her shoulders, her breasts... And as his mouth closed, hard and hot and hungry, over the tightened tip, still achingly sensitive from his attentions just a short time before, she felt the sting of desire speed along every nerve path, making her writhe restlessly against him.

'Joaquin...' she muttered again, but this time in open yearning, hungry demand rather than protest. 'Oh, dear Lord, Joaquin...'

And it all began again.

She had no idea what time they surfaced from the wild, erotic storm that had raged over them. She only knew that at some point Joaquin left their bed and went downstairs. He came back a short time later, carrying with him a tray laden down with plates of bread, cheese, fresh fruit and a bottle of one of the very best wines from his own vineyard, together with two beautiful, fine crystal goblets.

He fed her by hand, breaking off small pieces of bread or cheese, picking the finest grapes, the freshest apricots, and offering them to her as a mother might feed a child, so that all she had to do was to accept the delicacies from his hands. He held the glass to her mouth, tilting it so that she could sip the rich red liquid, finally kissing away the faint stain that marked her lips with a gentleness that made her heart clench in sharp response.

When the simple meal was done, he put aside the tray, laying it on the table at the far side of the room, before coming back to take her hands in his, drawing her from the bed and taking her with him into the bathroom. There they showered together, Joaquin brushing the breadcrumbs from her skin, washing the faint stickiness of fruit juice from where it had dribbled onto her breasts. There too, inevitably, they made love yet again. This time with a slow, tantalising sensuality, that built up and up, taking them both totally out of themselves and into a world where nothing mattered but their bodies, their touch, their kisses, and the heat that flamed between them. And ultimately that heat, that passion pushed them over the edge into a pulsing, shuddering climax that drained what little was left of even Joaquin's strength and left them with barely enough energy to make the brief journey from the shower to the bed before they tumbled headlong into the total oblivion of a sleep so deep it was like unconsciousness.

They had barely spoken a word to each other all night, Cassie reflected now. Talking hadn't been needed; it had seemed superfluous. They had let their bodies, their hands, their mouths, their senses do all the contacting that was necessary and they had communicated on such a basic, primitive level that there had been no need of words at all!

But that had been then, and this was now, she told herself uncomfortably. Last night had been an experience enclosed in a bubble, a moment out of time. A time when she had told herself that she would let things ride and not spoil what was happening by stirring up things that would only muddy the waters of their relationship.

Now she had to face those things, whether she liked it or not. Now she had to talk. There were things she had to ask Joaquin; things she needed to discuss with him, and she couldn't let it wait any longer.

But Joaquin wasn't in the bed beside her. The pillow still bore a dent where his head had rested, and the scent of his body lingered on the cover, in the sheets, but of the man himself there was no sign. A hasty check of the bathroom showed that it too was empty, something Cassie noted with an inward sense of relief.

Even though the room was cold and still, no trace of the steam and heat that had filled it last night, she still felt the echoes of the hungry coupling they had shared. The reverberations of the passionate climax still seemed to hang in the atmosphere, making her senses quiver, her nerves clenching in response, so that she hurried out of the bathroom, too uneasy to linger longer.

It was as she hurried back into the bedroom that the door opened quietly and Joaquin came in, the sight of him stopping her dead in surprise.

'Cassandra…'

His voice betrayed almost as much surprise as she was feeling. 'I thought you were still asleep.'

'You meant you hoped I was still asleep.'

The words were a mistake; she knew that as soon as she heard them hit the air. But she hadn't been able to hold them back.

It was the way he was dressed that had done it. The sleek, elegant suit and crisp shirt, even the tie that spoke of formality and discipline and—damn it—work!

'I didn't want to disturb you, that's true.'

Taking his cue from her, Joaquin was coolly formal. Not quite cold, but most definitely lacking in any warmth.

'I thought you might want to sleep in after…'

The way his eyes slid to the bed, and the gleam she had caught in them before they moved away from hers, sent prickles of irritation sparking along her spine. But what made the sparks turn into open flames of resentment was the faint but definitely triumphant edge to the sudden smile that curled up the corners of his mouth before he ruthlessly imposed a new control and determinedly forced them down again.

And that smile pushed her over the edge, into words that she knew were a mistake even as they left her mouth.

'After you had your way with me?' she snapped viciously, bringing his head up sharply, something much stronger than her own annoyance flaring in the darkness of his eyes.

'After we had our way *with each other*,' he corrected stiffly, the exotic notes of his accent contrasting stunningly with the cold crispness of each word.

'Whatever…' she forced herself to mutter ungraciously. If the truth were told, she much preferred to stay on the

side of righteous indignation, even if it wasn't actually jus-
tified. It felt more comfortable. And it seemed to square
better with an uneasy conscience.

She didn't want to feel this way, but she just wasn't
strong enough to stop herself.

One of the problems was the way that Joaquin was
dressed, and the physical effect that was having on her.

She had always adored the way he looked when—as she
had once put it—scrubbed and spruced up ready for work.
Apart from the fact that he looked stunning, the dark good
looks dramatically enhanced by the white shirt, every powerful line of his strong, lean body emphasised by the superb
fit and tailoring of his suit, she had never been able to resist
the appeal of the contrast between the controlled formality
of his clothing and the fiercely uninhibited, passionate man
she knew he really was underneath.

He had looked that way the very first time she had seen
him, cool and sleek and totally in control. She had been
working as a translator for an English wine importer who
had been negotiating a major deal with the Alcolar
Vineyards and who had asked her to attend this vital stage
of the negotiations to make sure he got everything quite
right. She had been sitting with her employer and his second in command at the huge, polished mahogany table in
the Alcolar boardroom when the door had opened and
Joaquin strode into the room.

It had seemed to Cassie as if the world had careered to
a halt, jolting her out of her sense of reality and into a place
where everything she had always believed in no longer had
any sway. She had looked, stared, blinked, unable to believe what she saw, looked again and from that moment
she hadn't been able to keep her eyes off him. It was as if
he were the most powerful magnet in the world and she
were some tiny, pin-fine compass needle. She was drawn
to him in an instant, held fast by the powerful pull of his

burning sexual appeal, and she had never been able to tug herself free ever since.

And Joaquin had been the same.

She could remember the moment he had been introduced, the sear of electricity up her arm as he'd taken her hand, the murmur of, *'Buenos dìas, senorita,'* in that stunningly accented voice. Their eyes had met, locked together, and it seemed that from then on she had never looked away again.

But she must have done, because somehow the meeting had gone on, and the deal had been struck. She didn't know if her employer had got the terms he'd wanted, or if Joaquin had arranged things his way, her concentration on the matter in hand so totally shot that it had been a miracle she had been able to translate at all. She only knew that when she'd spoken those jet-black eyes had been drawn to her face, fixing on it and watching her so intently that she'd actually feared that his gaze might mark her face, bruising it faintly where his eyes had rested. At first she had thought that he had been concentrating on following her translation; it was only much later that she'd learned that Joaquin Alcolar spoke English almost as well as she did herself, and that he would have been perfectly capable of conducting the meeting in his second language, if he had chosen to do so.

'So you concede that it was not just me forcing my wicked attentions on you.'

Joaquin's sharply enunciated words slashed into her memories like a sword slicing through silk, forcing her back to the present with an abruptness that had her blinking in unfocused confusion.

'I—yes—of course…' she managed, hoping she was answering what he had really said and not just what she thought she had heard.

She really must concentrate. This was too important just to let drift.

'I—it was mutual,' she managed hastily and saw his brusque nod of satisfaction, though none of the worrying expression in his eyes eased in any way.

'I'm glad to hear that,' he commented cynically. 'I have never forced a woman yet and I certainly do not intend to start with you.'

He didn't have to, and well he knew it, Cassie told herself. If anything offended him it was the thought she might just be implying that his seduction technique was not the carefully honed skill that it was. The number of women, all of them beautiful, successful and rich, nearly as beautiful and rich as he was himself, who had passed through his life from the time that he had reached adulthood attested to his almost legendary prowess with the opposite sex, and he wasn't likely to want to see that reputation threatened in any way.

'No, I'm not claiming you forced me.'

'Then what the hell is the matter with you?'

Joaquin was having a hard time adjusting to the woman he had discovered since he had come back into the room. He had left his bed reluctantly this morning, only forced out of it by the knowledge that there were business matters he had to deal with. Business matters that wouldn't wait. And so, in spite of the fact that both his hungry body and his deepest instincts had been demanding that he stayed right where he was, taking Cassandra into his arms and kissing her softly awake, stern common sense and duty had forced him to get up and head for the shower.

He should have gone straight to work after that, aiming to reach his office well before the heat of the day really kicked in and made conditions much less tolerable. But he hadn't been able to resist coming back into the bedroom to see Cassandra one more time before he left.

Only to find that she was no longer the softly sensual sleeper he had left curled up in the bed, as if still feeling his presence beside her. Instead she had turned back into the woman he had been having so much trouble with over the past weeks. The woman who was edgy, touchy, sharp-tongued and impossible to understand. The woman whose moods were difficult to predict, whose mind seemed so often to be elsewhere, lost in thoughts he couldn't discover.

'I thought—'

'You thought that because we'd had a—a hot night—that I would be quite content to lie here, stark naked, and just wait for my lord and master to come back and take up from where we left off?'

'Yes—no! Well—what the devil would be wrong with that?'

Okay, so he hadn't *expected* her to lie there and wait for him, but he certainly wasn't going to object to the idea of it! But how he wished she hadn't said 'stark naked'. He'd been aware of the fact that she had no clothes on, of course. No red-blooded male could look at that luscious body and not be aware of that. But they were often naked with each other, usually totally comfortably, and he was trying to be relaxed about it.

But the words *stark naked*, together with the implication of her just lying there, combined with heated memories of the night before, had served to scramble his brain. That was rubbing his nose in things, reducing his thought processes from efficient to single-minded so that they could run on only one track. And a very basic one at that—one that was in no way conducive to holding a rational argument with an illogically furious woman who was standing right in front of him stark damn naked!

'What the devil…?' Cassandra repeated, the words rushing through her teeth on a violent breath. 'Do you really think that I would be prepared to do that?'

'Well, you are still here in my room,' Joaquin pointed out, 'Waiting for me. And…'

He let his eyes drop, his gaze skimming over the soft curves, the slender limbs exposed to him, the shadow of curls between her legs. He immediately recognised his mistake as his body subjected him to a sharp, stinging twist of desire that changed the fit of his trousers from comfortable to way too tight in the space of a heartbeat.

'And you are naked,' he muttered, roughly, struggling with the feeling.

Cassandra's reaction disturbed him.

For the first time since they had been together, she looked totally shocked, embarrassed at realising that she was wearing no clothes. Her hands came up to cross over her chest, her eyes darkening, and her mouth actually fell open slightly in horror. Not even on the first time they had slept together had she looked like this. This was new. And it was something he didn't like at all.

'Here…'

Reaching for the nearest thing to hand, he flung the black cotton robe at her.

'Put that on.'

As she scrambled into the concealing garment, her haste betraying the way she was feeling, he had to admit to himself that he didn't know whether he had offered her the robe to ease her evident embarrassment or to soothe his own disturbed state of mind. He just couldn't think straight with her standing there before him. Totally nude. Indignation had put a spark in her eyes, brought a rush of blood to the surface of her skin—even her body was washed with the flush of pink—and it was damnably distracting.

In spite of the fact that she obviously wished it weren't, her nakedness was pure provocation to any living, breathing male. Everything that was masculine in him urged him to respond in the most primitive, basic way. But he knew from Cassandra's expression that to do so would be the most foolish move he could make.

So he had to get her covered up—and fast! And the black robe was the only thing he could find.

Not that it really helped, he acknowledged a moment

later as Cassandra pulled the soft cotton firmly round herself, belting it tightly at her waist. The robe was his and it totally swamped her, coming almost to her ankles, the sleeves hanging way down at the ends of her arms, the wrap-over front gaping loosely at her throat and revealing the beginning of the curves of her breasts. In its own way, the item of clothing was a whole new form of torture, making her look even more feminine and vulnerable, emphasising the fragility of her bones at ankle and wrist, the slender, satin-skinned lines of her neck.

But it was the look in her eyes that stung so sharply.

'*Maldito sea!*' he muttered violently as she tied another knot in the belt for good measure. 'There's no need to act as if just my look will contaminate you!'

The dark savagery in his tone brought her head up, her eyes widening in shock. He supposed he should explain that his anger was more at himself, and the conflict that was going on between his brain and his groin, than at her. But the truth was that he didn't think he could put it into words. And besides, he didn't want to. He didn't want to try to explain something that he really didn't understand himself. Didn't want to reveal raw, unformed thoughts when he had no idea at all what her response might be.

'I—I wasn't thinking that.'

'No—then what were you thinking, *querida*?'

He laced the term of affection with an acid that turned it into something the exact opposite of loving.

'Why should my seeing your body—the body I have seen, touched, *kissed* a thousand times before now—why should that suddenly turn into a crime?'

'I never said that!'

'No, but you sure as hell implied it!'

His eyes raked over her now carefully concealed body and he didn't trouble to try and hide the hot anger that was forcing its way up through his control, like lava pushing through the surface of a volcano, and pouring out down the sides.

'But don't you think that it's a little too late to suddenly turn prim and proper? You weren't so coy about being with me last night.'

'Last night was last night!' Cassandra flung at him, blue eyes flashing defiance. 'It was different!'

'Different how?' he demanded. 'And today is—what? A time for second thoughts?'

Her inability to answer, the way that her eyes dropped away from his, almost destroyed him. Holding on tight to what little was left of his shattered self-control, he forced himself to speak through lips that might have been carved from wood, they felt so stiff and unresponsive.

'I thought you enjoyed it!'

The need to fight the heavily erotic images that his brain was throwing at him, and the knowledge that his body was reacting hard and fast to just the thought of the things he remembered, the things he had done, the things he would love to do again, loosened his control over his tone. The comment came out harder, coarser than he had ever planned, and to judge from Cassandra's face that was what she felt too.

'And enjoyment is everything?'

Blazing defiance burned in her eyes, warning him that he had well overstepped the line, wherever the line that she now laid down might be.

'It's a pretty damn important part of things!' he tossed at her in furious exasperation. 'I never heard you complain before!'

'And because I never complained, that means that nothing is wrong?'

'Cassie, if you mean to complain about something—then at least do me the courtesy of letting me know what I'm accused of.'

Cassie. There it was again, Cassie thought. There was

Joaquin's own particular usage of the shortened form of her name. The one that warned, that spoke ominously of danger to come.

Just the thought of it dried her mouth, shrivelling all hope of an answer into ashes on her tongue. She couldn't find a word to say to him, no way of broaching the fears that burned so sharply in her mind that she was afraid he might be able to look into her eyes and read them there.

'Well, Cassie?' Joaquin asked, the smile that accompanied the words sending a cold, creeping shiver down the length of her spine. 'Nothing to say? Nothing to *complain* about?'

What could she say? She had to say *something*. But with Joaquin in this mood, this dangerous, alien, disturbing mood, she didn't dare just launch into the real reasons for the way she was feeling.

'You're going to work!' she blustered and heard his short, harsh bark of totally sceptical laughter.

'I'm going to work,' he endorsed cynically. 'As I do nearly every day. Is there a problem with that?'

'I...'

Cassie pulled the edges of the robe closer together over her breasts, feeling even more than ever the desperate need to hide away from his burning, searching eyes and the way they were fixed on her face, seeming to probe right into her soul.

'I didn't think you would—at least not today.'

Coward! she reproached herself. If she was honest, then today was not what mattered—but Friday. The anniversary of the day they had first come together. That was what was really important to her.

'And why particularly not today?'

Abruptly Joaquin swung away, pushing his hands deep into his trouser pockets as he paced across the floor to the window and back. And then back again. Then just as Cassie, unable to bear the resemblance to the restless prowling of a sleek, caged, restless jungle cat, feared her tongue might run away with her, he suddenly whirled round again and looked deep into her unhappy eyes.

'Oh, I see—because of last night? You didn't want me to go because…'

'I thought we needed to talk!' Cassie rushed in, desperate to try and bring the conversation round to the topic of their future. Clearly Joaquin simply thought that all she wanted was a long, luxurious day in bed, and that was not at all the way she wanted things to go.

'And I have to work. If you recall, I came home to work yesterday, but I didn't get the work I had planned done, did I?'

And whose fault was that? the look in his eyes, the faint curve to his mouth, demanded. Who had distracted him, seducing him away from his desk with the enticement of her body? Who had offered sex instead of work?

'You don't need to work,' Cassie muttered mutinously.

If he never worked again, it wouldn't matter. The wine business was so firmly established, so hugely profitable, that he could appoint a manager, sit back and enjoy a luxurious income for the rest of his life. She admired the fact that he *did* work, that he didn't just live the life of a playboy, but right now she wasn't prepared to concede that. She wanted to get her point across and, feeling the way she did, she would argue that black was white if that was what was needed to win her case.

'I want to work.'

Joaquin's tone had hardened, and the half-smile that had been on his face a moment before had vanished like mist before sun. It was only when she saw how bleak and icy his expression looked without it that Cassie realised just how much easier, more approachable that smile had made him look and found herself wishing for it back.

She was suddenly desperately, painfully aware of the fact that she might have lived with this man for almost a year, but she didn't really know him at all. Deep down, there was a dark, buried part of him that he kept hidden from her.

'I have a lot to get done before Friday. You know Friday is a very important day.'

Oh, she knew that all right. But was he thinking of it as important for the same reasons she was?

CHAPTER FOUR

GIVING in to cowardice, Cassie decided she was no longer so sure she wanted to risk finding out. Never ask questions you don't want to know the answers to, her mother always said. And there was one answer to this that she did not want to hear at all.

'Friday?' she asked, trying to distract herself with a glance in the mirror and grimacing in distaste as she saw the way she looked.

Swamped by the black robe that was designed for Joaquin's tall, masculine frame and not her own feminine one, and with her blonde hair tangled into an appalling bird's nest, she looked a wreck, nothing like the elegant professional woman who had first caught Joaquin's eye at that first business meeting.

She was going to ask him if they had a future together, looking like *this*? Where was her pride? Her self-esteem?

Reaching for her hairbrush, she started to pull it through her hair, wincing sharply as it caught in a particularly tight knot.

'Why is Friday so important?'

She knew she was prevaricating, delaying the moment and the question that would decide her fate. If she really had to ask it? Couldn't she give it a miss just for today? Couldn't they go on as they were for a little while yet? Have one more night like last night?

'What's happening then?'

'I'm meeting the buyers from London—*we're* meeting the buyers from London,' Joaquin amended.

'We?' Cassie echoed, frowning her confusion at his reflection in the mirror. 'You want me to be there?'

'Of course—you're my interpreter.'

'But they're English! You don't need an interpreter for them! You speak perfect English—quite possibly better than some of them!'

Joaquin's grin was wide and wicked, a flash of brilliantly white teeth in his darkly tanned face.

'I know that and you do too. But I don't necessarily want them to know that. At least, not at this stage of the game. I would prefer them to think that I might not understand everything they say. That way they might not be quite so guarded in their opinions—they might let something slip.'

'Something you can use to your advantage?'

'*Obviamente*. What else?'

What else? Cassie asked herself privately. What else would Joaquin be thinking of but business? What else would matter to him as much as making money, wheeling and dealing?

Why was she fooling herself even trying to hope that he might have something more personal, more emotional on his mind?

Her hair was almost brushed smooth now. Every tangle had been tugged out of it and it was no longer a bird's nest. But it looked as flat and as limp as she felt deep inside.

To her horror hot tears stung at her eyes and she blinked hard to fight them back, slowly turning to face Joaquin where he stood in the middle of the room, eyes dark, a faint frown on his face, his hands pushed deep into the pockets of his trousers.

'So you want me to come and sit in on a business meeting on Friday?'

'A business dinner,' Joaquin corrected. 'We're taking them out to dinner in the evening—now what the hell was that look for?'

'What look?' Cassie tried to hedge, though she knew from his dark scowl that it hadn't worked.

He had always been able to see right through her when

she tried to avoid telling him the truth. That was why she had had such a terrible time keeping the way she was feeling from him just lately. For once she had had cause to be thankful that he was a workaholic. When he was out of the house, she could let her mask slip, admit to the fears she was facing about the future.

'What look?' Joaquin echoed, lacing the words with dark mockery.

He strode across the room towards her, catching hold of her shoulders and spinning her round so that she faced the mirror once more. When she tried to avoid looking at her own reflection, afraid of what she might see, he caught her chin firmly between hard finger and thumb and turned her face so that she couldn't do anything else.

'That look! The one that tells me I have committed some appalling sin, one for which I should beg forgiveness on my knees before you, clad in sackcloth and ashes.'

'Oh, now you're being ridiculous!'

'Am I?' Joaquin questioned darkly. 'Am I really? Look at yourself, Cassie—look!' he commanded when she stubbornly struggled to avert her face, not wanting to meet her own eyes in the glass.

Cassie knew what she saw—but what was it that Joaquin saw in her face? Was it really possible that he could have misinterpreted her expression? That where she saw eyes clouded by anxiety, and a face that struggled to hide the pain and fear she had lived with for days, he saw something else? Something that made him think she was angry and distant from him? That she was the one whose mood was likely to prove difficult and disruptive?

Right now, feeling as vulnerable as she did, just the idea seemed like a welcome relief. Clearly the thought that their all-important anniversary was coming up meant little to him. Less than little—nothing at all! He'd even arranged a business meeting for the day. And wanted her to act as his *employee*!

'Do you know what day it is on Friday?'

His reaction was so swift, so revealing that it tore at her heart. His head went back, very slightly, his eyes narrowing. And then there was a total blanking out of his expression, all trace of *anything* wiped from his features so that they were as smooth and unrevealing as those of a marble statue, the dark eyes as opaque as the unseeing sockets in a carved head.

'Of course I know what day it is. The day we met—a year ago.'

'Then...'

'Oh, I see—I'm supposed to go the whole sentimental road, am I? Flowers and chocolates?'

He was taunting her now, provoking deliberately, she knew, but she couldn't stop herself from rising to the provocation. Besides, it was probably so much better than letting him see how devastated she really was deep inside.

'Well, I'd expected *something*!'

Was that cold, tight little voice really hers?

'What I get is a business meeting! And, what's more, a business meeting at which I'm supposed to be working!'

'That meeting has been arranged for a long time.'

'Oh, I'll just bet it has!'

And she should know exactly what came first in Joaquin's mind. Business first and foremost every time. No matter what else might be involved.

'And even if it hadn't, you wouldn't cancel it.'

'No.'

It was cold and flat and totally unmovable. Of course.

'I couldn't cancel it even if I wanted to.'

'And you don't want to.'

'No.'

Damn the woman, what had got into her lately? He never knew which Cassandra would be waiting for him when he got home. Never knew if the Cassandra who had so enchanted and enthralled him from the start would be there, or the difficult, moody, bad-tempered creature who seemed to have taken her place for the past few weeks. The first Cassandra would have understood that this meeting had been set up months ago and even if he wanted to get out of it, there was no way that he could.

This Cassandra didn't seem to understand very much at all. Let alone the fact that he had been working so hard lately in order to give himself some space, some time to try to get things sorted out in his mind.

'Look, I know exactly what day it is on Friday—but it's not as if we have something worth celebrating. If we'd been married it might have been different...'

Her reaction showed how much she disliked his words. Her head went back, her face stiffening. Her eyes seemed darker, sharper, colder, and even the soft fullness of her mouth seemed to have thinned and tightened as if holding back something bitter and harsh that she really wanted to say.

'Is that it?' he demanded abruptly. 'Is that what you want? Is it marriage you're after?'

If it was possible, she looked even more appalled. Horrified.

'Marriage I'm... No!'

She shook her head, sending her blonde hair flying as she emphasised the word.

'No!' she said again, tossing her brush down onto the rumpled surface of the bed to reinforce the statement. 'No way! Never! If you're thinking that I wanted you to go down on one knee and beg me to marry you, then think again.'

So he'd been heading down the wrong road with thoughts like that, Joaquin admitted to himself. He didn't know whether the feeling that rushed through him was one of relief or savage regret at the thought that he had obviously been so completely wrong. Yesterday he would have said that relief would be uppermost. Today he was not so sure.

'I told you I don't do commitment!' he growled awkwardly.

'And when did I ever ask you for any such thing?'

'Then we both understand each other.'

'Perfectly,' Cassandra tossed at him, moving to the wardrobe and yanking open the door, staring fixedly inside as she decided what to wear for the day.

'Bueno!'

'Yes, *bueno*!' she muttered into the wardrobe. 'We're both on the same track for once.'

Now relief was very definitely the most forceful feeling he was experiencing. Total, overwhelming, undiluted relief that he hadn't opened himself up to her.

He couldn't believe that he had come so close to saying something damned stupid. Something she really didn't want. Something like. I don't do commitment, but for you...

For you *what*?

If he'd started that sentence, then how the hell would he have finished it?

He didn't know. He couldn't even have said to himself what he felt—except that right now what he had with this woman was something he wanted to hold onto.

For ever? He didn't know. He didn't believe in a forever kind of love. He might have done once—as a child, he would have said that he wanted the sort of marriage that his parents had: perfect, loving faithful. Then, when he was fifteen, he'd found out that that marriage was just an illusion. His father had been unfaithful not once, but twice. And he had a son from each relationship.

Even worse, he had learned that the relationship that had resulted in his own birth and that of his sister had never truly been founded on love, but on duty and expediency, the need to have an heir for the family business, and hard, cold, financial facts.

He had seen his mother's devastated face, heard her crying in her bed, heard the rows that had raged in the stillness of the night. He had stopped believing in love and commitment and for ever. And nothing that had happened since then had changed his mind.

If anything, his own experience had reinforced the belief he had come to in those long-ago nights. He was his father's son. Like Juan Alcolar, he wasn't made for a long-term, exclusive, faithful relationship. No woman he had known had lasted more than a year. He had tired of them and moved on, without even a backward glance, and that had suited him fine.

But he wasn't tired of this one. No way.

And last night had proved that with a vengeance!

But what about Cassandra? That was a question he had no answer to. Just lately he hadn't known what her mood would be, couldn't guess at what she was thinking—feeling. She seemed restless and unsettled. It had crossed his mind more than once that perhaps *she* was ready to move on.

That perhaps she had already found someone else.

But no—if she had, would last night have been so devastating? So overwhelmingly sensual? Surely if her mind, her heart were already straying, she couldn't have responded to him in that way?

'So we are in agreement?'

'Mmm...'

Cassandra's head was buried in the wardrobe and as she pulled out a dress whatever she had said in response was hopelessly muffled.

'Neither of us wants more than we already have?' Joaquin continued, feeling as if he were inching his way through shark-infested water, not at all sure what he might find. 'What we agreed on from the start?'

'No ties, no commitment...'

Cassandra's attention was on the dress, checking it over with what he privately considered excessive care.

'*Exacto!*'

His tone brought her eyes to his face in a rush and just for a moment he wondered... But then she smiled and nodded emphatically.

'Exactly!' she confirmed, her voice as firm and unwavering as her wide-eyed gaze. 'That's what you offered from the start. You were always straight with me. Have I ever asked for more?'

'No.'

Joaquin flashed her a quick, wide grin, using it to hide the maelstrom of feeling inside.

'That's why we fit together so well—why I'm so comfortable with you. You don't want any more than I can give.'

'No,' Cassandra said, an odd, strangled note in her voice. 'No, I don't want anything more than you can give.'

Her eyes moved away from his, glancing at the clock on the bedside table, and when she spoke again that odd, inexplicable note had vanished, so totally that he was forced to wonder if it had ever been there at all. Or if, in fact, he had just imagined it.

'If you have to go to work, then you'd better get a move on,' she said unexpectedly casually, her previous annoyance at the prospect seeming to be forgotten. 'You don't want to be late.'

'I'll be back as soon as I can.'

Moving forward, he planted a quick, hard kiss on her lips, putting into it the relief he felt that, perhaps, after all they had moved past this difficult, uncomfortable stage and into clearer waters. To his surprise she didn't respond as fervently as she usually did, her mouth remaining stiff and unresponsive under his. Perhaps she wasn't over her annoyance as much as he had thought.

But he didn't have time to wonder, or to waste in any more argument. He really was going to be late if he didn't hurry. Tonight they could talk.

'I'll see you tonight,' he said. 'We'll continue where we left off…'

The swift, burning glance that swung from her face to the bed with its evidence of the passionate night they had shared left no doubt as to exactly what he meant. At least in bed they had no difficulty in communicating with the utmost clarity.

'Tonight,' he repeated, already heading for the door.

'Goodbye…'

Her reply was faint, cut off before it was completed as the door slammed to behind him.

'Goodbye…' Cassie repeated on a higher, quavering note, her voice breaking in the middle of the word. 'Goodbye, my love.'

Tears brimming in her eyes, she pressed her fingers to her mouth as if to crush down the kiss that he had left her with. It might be—had to be—the last kiss she would ever have from Joaquin and she wanted to hold onto it for as long as she possibly could, taste the faint lingering touch of his mouth on hers for as long as she could make it last.

She hadn't managed to ask her question outright. In the end she'd chickened out, cowardice and the sheer terror of knowing the truth holding her back and preventing her from speaking even though she had resolved to do so.

But she hadn't needed to speak. As it happened, Joaquin had answered the question completely and honestly, without her ever having to ask it.

'I told you I don't do commitment!'

'Neither of us wants more than we already have.'

'No ties, no commitment.'

'You don't want any more than I can give.'

What else did she need to know? How much clearer could Joaquin make things? He didn't see any real future for them together. Didn't want any more than what they already had. And it was obviously only by sheer luck that he hadn't already imposed his usual twelve-month-cut-off rule to what was left of their relationship.

No, not luck.

Recalling his last words, the way he had looked at her before he'd left, and the way his black-eyed gaze had gone to the bed, Cassie told herself miserably that she knew exactly why he hadn't imposed that cut-off rule yet.

Sex.

'We'll continue where we left off...'

And where they had left off was in bed. Making passionate love...

No! Not making love, but having hot, passionate sex. Hot passionate, *unemotional* sex.

That was it. That was all he saw between them. All he cared about. All he wanted.

It was not enough for her. It was not all she wanted. Very definitely not all she cared about.

And knowing it was all that he could offer was not something she could cope with.

She loved him so very much. And loving him so much, she couldn't endure being with him and knowing he felt nothing for her.

So she had to go.

She didn't want that either, but she had no choice. What Joaquin could give her was not enough to sustain her, or keep her heart happy in any way. It would kill her eventually. It would drain even the deep, deep well of love she had for him in the end. And it would destroy her more completely than leaving now would do.

If she left now, she would have less pain in the long run. It would be a clean, sharp, single blow—over and done with like an amputation. Like an amputation, the wound would scar over, in the end. It would never fully heal. There would always be a part of her, a large piece of her heart, that would be empty and damaged, but she would at least be able to function.

But if she stayed, she might end up totally destroyed, or, even worse, hating Joaquin so much that she set out to destroy him too.

So she had to go. Though she had nowhere to go to.

Now, while she still had the chance. While Joaquin was out of the way and wouldn't try to stop her. Because if he tried to stop her, for whatever reasons, then she knew she would give in and would lie down and let him walk all over her, emotionally at least. He would only have to say the single word, 'Stay,' and, fool that she was, she would stay, clinging on vainly to the hope that there would one day, in her dreams, be something more.

'And there never will be,' she sighed aloud. 'Never. He's made that quite clear.'

He couldn't have made it plainer if he'd tried. The axe might not be falling to sever their relationship right now, but she couldn't delude herself that it wouldn't fall, hard and fast, in the end when Joaquin decided that he had tired of her in bed too. He'd just about said as much, and, in pain and too scared to show it, she had reacted in instinctive panic. She had played a role, been colder, harder, more demanding than she would ever be capable of being in reality.

When Joaquin came home and found her gone, he would remember only that role. He would recall how she had been angry—at the fact that he wasn't celebrating their anniversary, he would believe. He would think that that was what had driven her to pack up and leave. It would never cross his mind to think that maybe, after all, she had been lying when she had said that she didn't want more than he could give.

Cassie shook her head despondently.

She hadn't been lying.

She *didn't* want from him anything more than he could

give—and give willingly and happily. If he couldn't give her his heart, his love, then she wasn't going to stay around, making it plain that she wanted, needed more, and making him uncomfortable because he didn't feel the way she longed for him to do.

No, she would go now, quietly and quickly, while he was out. She would take only the basic minimum of things she needed, and she would be gone before he came back. If she could just think of somewhere to go.

The sound of the telephone on the table beside the bed had her whirling and running to snatch it up, unexpected hope making her heart thud in fearful anticipation.

'Joaquin?'

Had he changed his mind? Rung back to say he was sorry—that he'd said all the wrong things—that what he wanted was to spend the day with her—and say...

But the voice at the other end of the line, although accented and deep, was not Joaquin's.

'Wrong brother, sweetheart,' Ramón drawled lightly. 'But I was looking for Joaquin, actually. Do I take it from your tone that he's not there with you?'

'No—no, he's not.'

And never likely to be again.

The truth hit home with a shock that turned Cassie's knees weak and had her sinking down onto the bed before they gave way completely.

'He's not here, Ramón. He went into work.'

She had thought that she had controlled her voice well enough. That she had erased the betraying tremor, the faint shadow of tears. But not well enough. Something had given her away, and Ramón had caught it.

'What's wrong, Cassie?' he demanded, his voice sharpening noticeably.

Cassie smoothed her hand over the crumpled pillow where Joaquin's dark head had rested just a short time before. The fine cotton was cool now, no heat from his body remaining, but the sheets still bore the lingering traces of the scent of his skin, and she inhaled hungrily, desperate to hold onto this one last physical memory of the man she loved.

'Cassie?' Ramón said again, more forcefully this time. 'What's happened?'

'It's—it's over, Ramón…'

She forced herself to say it though it tore at her heart, ripping it to shreds to hear the words aloud.

'We've broken up. No longer together—I—I'm leaving him.'

'What?'

Ramón swore violently in explosive Spanish.

'But I thought you guys were perfect together! Why the—? Oh—don't tell me—Joaquin and his damn one-year rule again? Is that it?'

'Something like that,' Cassie said sadly. It was close enough to the truth and she really didn't feel up to explaining the whole facts.

'The man's mad!' Joaquin's brother muttered. 'Crazy! But, Cassie—don't let him do this to you! You have to fight him…'

'No!' Cassie put in hastily, terrified that Ramón might make her want to weaken, that he might persuade her to stay. 'It's not Joaquin's decision—it's mine. I'm the one who's leaving.'

The silence at the other end of the phone line almost destroyed her. Ramón at a loss for words was as rare an event as Joaquin being in the same condition, and it was very nearly as devastating.

'You?'

'Joaquin was right, Ramón,' Cassie put in hastily. 'This relationship was only a one-year thing. We came to the end of the line—nowhere else to go.'

Nowhere that Joaquin was prepared to go anyway, she

told herself miserably, refusing even to look at the hope of what might have been.

'It's over, finished. I'm moving out today. I just need to find somewhere to stay until—'

Ramón didn't allow her to finish her sentence.

'I'll be round at once,' he said decisively, his tone making it clear there was no room for argument. 'I'll help you pack and then you can move in here with me.'

CHAPTER FIVE

COULD any week have lasted as long as this one? Cassie asked herself on a deep, despondent sigh as she poured herself a glass of cool, sparkling water, listening to the ice crackle as the liquid landed on top of it. Each day since she had left Joaquin and moved in to Ramón's apartment had felt as if it had lasted a lifetime.

A long, lonely, dreary, dragging lifetime. One that didn't seem to get any better, no matter how many times she tried to convince herself that it would.

And she had tried.

Every single night, as the darkness fell and she lay awake in the big comfortable bed she had told herself that tomorrow was another day. That tomorrow would be better. That it *had* to be better. How could it be any worse?

But each morning had dawned with the same dreary sense of dread, the same fearful anticipation of the long, weary hours that had to be got through until she could seek sanctuary in the darkness and the stillness once again. And each night she had lain awake again, staring blankly in front of her for yet more long, lonely hours, wishing with all her heart that she were back with Joaquin. That she had never left him.

When she slept, for the few hours she managed to sleep at all, she dreamed she was back there with him, back in the big house on the hill above the vineyard. Back in the room she and Joaquin had shared, in the bed where they had slept together. She would dream that he was with her, that she was curled tight against the hard power of his body, held comfortingly in the strength of his arms. And her dreams were so real, so vivid, so intense that she would wake believing it was real, with every nerve awake to the closeness of the man she loved, her whole body on fire with a hunger and a need of him that came from some deep, primitive part of her soul.

She would sigh, stretch, reach out for him…

And of course he wasn't there.

With the terrible, jolting sense of awareness of the truth would come a devastating sense of loss and shock. She would lie there, aching and empty, hungry and yearning so desperately for him that she would curl up on herself with a moan of pain. The tears would slide from her eyes, impossible to hold back, and seep into the pillow so that every morning the wet patches were silent testimony to the misery of the night.

The sound of a car pulling up outside gave her despondent spirits a tiny, feeble lift.

Ramón was home. That at least meant that she would have someone else to talk to, someone to distract her. Someone to help her stay put right here and withstand the temptation to turn round and head back to the house she had shared with Joaquin.

At least once every day, and frequently more often, she had found the temptation to head for the door and drive out to the big white house by the vineyard almost irresistible.

What harm could it do? a persistent little voice inside her head kept asking.

She knew only too well what harm would result. She had said goodbye to Joaquin, in her mind, if not in her heart, and if she was to see him again then she would lose all the strength that she had gained from the week she had spent away from him.

Like an addict faced with the prospect of a free fix, she wouldn't be able to stop herself from reaching out and taking it, and the result would be destruction to her hopes of eventually gaining some sort of peace of mind. If she saw Joaquin, she would end up going back to him. It was as inevitable as the sun rising over Spain tomorrow morning. And if she went back to him, she was only storing up the prospect of bitter pain at some point in the probably not too distant future. Joaquin had made it plain that he was not looking for anything permanent with her, or for any form of commitment. Going back to him wouldn't change that. It would only delay, not prevent, the inevitable.

The sound of the bell ringing pierced her unhappy thoughts, bringing her head up sharply. When it was followed by a persistent thumping on the thick wooden door to Ramón's apartment, she smiled, shaking her head in disbelief at Ramón's impatience.

'Typical Alcolar!' she laughed. 'Can't wait for anything!'

So like his brother. The unwanted reminder slipped into her mind, sobering her immediately. But then as the thumping sounded again she tightened the belt on the robe she had slipped into for comfort after taking a long shower to wash off the heat of the day, and headed out into the shadowy hallway.

'What happened, Ramón?' she asked, slipping the catch and pulling the big, heavy door open. 'Did you forget your key, love?'

'Ramón, you *have* to tell me if you know where the hell she is…'

The words, raw, harsh and strongly accented, spoken in a very masculine voice, clashed with her own as her eyes fell on the man who stood outside the apartment. The one man she most wanted to see and yet had prayed she would never, ever encounter again because it would destroy her.

Joaquin Alcolar in the devastatingly attractive flesh. And just one swift glance at his dark, stunning features undid all the hard work of the week as she had known it would do, leaving her hopelessly weak and totally vulnerable, a prey to all the uncontrollable, utterly irrepressible emotions that rose up from deep inside her heart.

'I've tried every damn place I can think of to look and...'

Belatedly becoming aware of her dazed silence, Joaquin stopped dead too, his black eyes going to her shocked face, and narrowing in swift, stunned response.

'You!' he muttered, the single word sounding as if it had been forced from a painfully dry throat.

'No!'

Cassie's reaction was swift, purely instinctive. Acting through fear, totally beyond thought, she moved immediately to close the door, wanting to slam it shut in his face before he could have any further effect on her. Before Joaquin could realise just what effect his appearance had already had.

But she never managed to complete the action.

Fast as a striking snake, Joaquin's hand came out, slamming hard against the wood of the door and stopping it in mid-curve. For a couple of silent, awkward seconds the two of them faced each other, Cassie struggling to complete the closing of the door and Joaquin determined to prevent her. At first it seemed as if they were almost equally matched, but then Joaquin exerted just a little more pressure, used a little more strength, and Cassie gave way, falling back with a small cry of despair and panic as the big, dark, threatening figure of the man moved inexorably into the room.

'Go away!'

It was all she could manage and she knew it was hopeless and totally ineffectual even before he turned on her a blazing look that was so filled with arrogance and scorn that it dismissed her feeble attempt at protest with as much ease as he might flick away a fly that had landed on his arm.

'No chance! I'm not leaving till I find out just what is going on.'

'But—wha-what are you doing here? Why—?'

'Oh, no, *querida*,' Joaquin cut in brutally. 'That is *my* question.'

Kicking the door to behind him with a slam that made

her wince in nervous distress, he raked burning eyes from the top of her loose blonde hair, over the pale green silky robe, and down to where her narrow, bare feet rested on the polished wooden floor, toes curled slightly, apparently poised, ready to run if necessary.

'I have to ask you what the hell you are doing here, in my brother's apartment—and dressed like *that*.'

Cassie knew that the robe was fastened firmly across her breasts, but still, when subjected to the cruel scrutiny of those molten eyes, she felt as if the flimsy protection of the delicate material had been torn away from her, leaving her dangerously exposed and vulnerable.

'I—I live here now...' she managed shakily, pulling the front of the garment even tighter across her chest, and undoing and then retying the belt in a jerky, nervous movement, more for something to do rather than because it actually needed adjusting.

'Oh, do you?'

The question scorched across her already sensitised nerves, making her shiver inwardly at the ominous undercurrents that lurked in the depths of his tone, totally at odds with the simple words. They made her think of rocks with jagged edges and unwary boats, torn to pieces, sinking under the weight of water that poured in through holes ripped in their sides.

'Yes. Yes, I do.'

This time she dragged up a touch of defiance from somewhere, injecting it into her tone with an effort. But all the rebellion drained right out of her again as a cynical dark eyebrow lifted, expressing deep contempt without a word needing to be spoken.

'I've moved in with Ramón,' she declared, pushing the words between them like a shield against him—or against her own most foolish impulses.

It was impossible to think clearly—to think at all. She only wanted him to turn and walk out of here, to go, before she did something really stupid, like fling herself into his arms, telling him that she loved him and if he would only take her back...

I've moved in with Ramón.

The words flared behind Joaquin's eyelids, searing themselves into his brain, blinding him, destroying all hope of thinking rationally.

I've moved in with Ramón.

Did she mean—she couldn't mean what he thought! She didn't...

But then he remembered the time, just over a week ago. The time when he had arrived home unexpectedly.

Cassandra had been in a strange mood that day. Jittery as a cat on hot bricks and obviously on edge.

And then Ramón had turned up, using *her* key, obviously expected—and she had smiled, her whole face lighting up...

Ramón, who had a habit of turning up out of the blue. He had done that years before and claimed to be—had been proved to be—his father's son by another woman. The woman Juan Alcolar had said that he loved, while his legitimate son's mother had been just a marriage of duty, of convenience. That revelation had destroyed Joaquin's own belief in love and honesty and fidelity.

In any sort of happy ever after.

And now Cassandra. His Cassandra. His woman.

I've moved in with Ramón.

It couldn't be true. It *couldn't*! But why else would she say it? Why else would she be here, in that flimsy slip of a robe, obviously waiting for, expecting Ramón?

When she moved it was blatantly evident that underneath the robe she was wearing nothing at all. Her breasts swung softly, unfettered by any bra, and the smooth line of her hips...

He clenched his teeth together savagely, biting back the vicious outburst he wanted to fling in her face. His breath hissed between them as he struggled to get the worst of his black rage under control enough to speak.

'You are living here—with my brother? You have been here all this time? While I was looking for you?'

She swallowed hard, seemed unable to speak, but there was no doubting the firmness of her nod of affirmation, the way those blue eyes clashed with his as she destroyed any remaining hope with a single gesture.

'I see…'

Oh, he saw all right. And what he saw burned in his soul like acid, eating away at him deep inside.

'So tell me, when did this happen?'

He was proud of that tone. It sounded almost cool, calm, in contrast to the lava-like fury that was boiling up inside him.

'It's obviously a very sudden thing.'

'Not really—it's been coming for a while.'

'And you didn't think to say anything?'

How the hell had he not noticed?

But of course he had. He had seen that something was wrong. It had been obvious that she'd been uneasy, edgy with him, never quite herself. But he had never imagined this.

And what the hell was *herself*? What was the real Cassandra? The true woman? The woman he'd known— thought he'd known…

'I did try—but…'

'You tried!'

The disgust he felt rang in his voice.

'Oh, yes, lady, you *tried*. You tried *so* hard. You complained that I was going to work. Said that you didn't want to act as my interpreter on Friday—well, you sure as hell got out of that one! By Friday you had disappeared from my life and I had no idea where on earth you were! You'd gone and all you left was that bloody note!'

He swung away from her, pacing the length of the room

and back again, his eyes glazed, blurring his vision as he relived the night, a week before, when he had returned home to the empty room. An empty room in a still, silent, empty house.

He had called her name, thinking that she was perhaps by the pool or out in the garden. But there had been no answer. And so he had waited. He had set some wine to chill and he had sprawled on a lounger by the pool—the lounger on which they had made love the night before—and he had waited.

And waited.

And waited.

He had spent a long time thinking over the events of the previous night. Reviewing the things they had said to each other that morning. He had faced the fact that he was, after all, in deeper than he'd thought. Far deeper than he had ever believed was possible. That he had finally met the woman he couldn't walk away from.

He'd looked at the decision he'd made during the day and known it was the only way open to him. He still hadn't known if he believed in for ever, only that for this woman he had to give it a try. He'd taken out the ring that he'd bought, spending hours at a jeweller's when he should have been at meetings. And he had struggled with a sensation that he had experienced only rarely in his life before.

Fear.

The fear that Cassandra might not feel the same way. That her change of mood, her strange behaviour over the past weeks had meant that *she* was the one who was preparing to turn her back on *him*. That she was the one who was about to walk. And as the time had dragged on and she hadn't appeared, that fear had grown worse and worse.

It was when he had come inside again that he had found the note, tucked between two photograph frames on the mantelpiece, in a way that was such a cliché it would have been blackly humorous if it hadn't been for what it had contained.

That note had taken all his worst possible fear and turned it dark as night.

'"I'm sorry it had to be this way",' he quoted cynically now, '"but it's over." And that was it. Not even a dozen words. Would it have killed you to say why?'

Cassandra flinched. She actually flinched away at his words, the sound of his anger. He couldn't believe that she was shocked at his vehemence, surprised by his fury.

What the hell else had she expected?

Bitter memories surfaced. Memories of the night before she had left him, the delight he had felt in her then, the passion they had shared.

'You gave no sign, woman. We slept together that night...'

He knew he didn't have to say which night. The way her head went back, the brief moment in which she closed her eyes, the way her face whitened, all told him without speaking that his words had hit home.

'We made love...'

But that brought her eyes open again in a rush, blazing into his in rejection of what he had said.

'No, we didn't! We did no such thing! We—we had sex...'

'Sex—yeah.'

Hearing the way she said it, the use of the basic, blunt term instead of any gentler euphemism, told him just what she had felt about it. All that it had meant to her. The thought burned like acid in his guts.

He knew where Ramón kept the alcohol in his apartment and he headed over to the cupboard, pulling out a bottle of brandy and wrenching open the top of it with a vicious movement. Sloshing an unmeasured amount into a fine crystal glass, he lifted it, tilting it in Cassie's direction in a mockery of a toast, before taking a deep swallow of the fiery liquid.

'Yeah, we had sex,' he went on savagely. 'Good sex—the best!'

He turned blazing dark eyes on Cassie's ashen face, fury etched onto his face.

'Don't you dare to try to deny that, my darling!'

'I—wouldn't,' she managed to whisper, raw and husky. 'I couldn't...'

'No, you couldn't, *mi belleza*,' he tossed back at her. 'You most definitely could not. Not unless you are also going to claim to be the greatest actress the world has known. Remember I was there with you every inch of the way that night. I know how you felt; how you responded to me. You were there beneath me; I was with you, holding you, *inside* you! You can't convince me that you weren't out of your mind with wanting me—needing me...'

'Yes—*yes*! I mean no...'

Cassie's hands flew up and outward in a desperate gesture to cut him off when he would have raged on.

'No, I can't pretend I didn't want you—I never have. I told you at the time that it was mutual.'

'And yet less than twenty-four hours later, you had packed your bags and moved out—running from me—running here—to—to Ramón.'

In his mind he was seeing the day that Ramón had come to the *finca*, recalling the welcoming smile on her face, the way she had encouraged him into the house. Hell, she had even given him her keys!

The flare of hot jealousy hazed his eyes with red, blinding him as his hand clenched tight on the glass.

'After what we shared.'

'I told you at the time that there was more to it than enjoyment—than sex.'

'And Ramón gives you this more?'

'Right now, he gives me something that you never did!'

Her voice had lost something of the firmness it had held only moments before. Something he had said had struck home, shaking her conviction, rocking the foundations they were built on. But what? Which particular sentence had hit the target, thudding into the red, if not precisely into the gold?

There was something not quite right about this situation. Something he couldn't completely work out—but every instinct he possessed told him that something was wrong. Something that raised all the tiny hairs on the back of his neck in warning like the hackles on a wary dog. But the haze of bitterness and shock, the raw agony of disbelief, clouded his brain so that thinking clearly was an impossibility.

Joaquin lifted the brandy bottle again, waving it in Cassie's direction, lifting one eyebrow questioningly.

'Join me in a drink?'

'No—and do you think you should?'

'Think I should?' Joaquin echoed cynically. 'Why not? After all, if my brother can steal my woman from me then surely I am entitled to help myself to some of his brandy in return.'

'Steal your woman?' Cassie repeated, actually managing to look convincingly bemused. 'What are you talking about?'

'"I've moved in with Ramón",' Joaquin quoted at her, considering the brandy bottle, then abruptly setting it down again. 'You're living with my brother.'

'You knew that already! I told you…'

The shocking sense of realisation was like a blow to her face, stunning her into silence, shrivelling the words on her tongue.

Too late she realised how he was interpreting her reply. How he was putting far too much into it.

Not 'you're living with my brother', as in you share this

apartment with Ramón, but you're living *with* Ramón. As she had once lived with Joaquin himself.

'No,' she tried but Joaquin wasn't listening.

'You said you were fine with what we had—that you didn't want anything more.'

He slammed his half-empty glass down on the table, heedless of the way that the rich amber brandy slopped over the side.

'Then Ramón—my brother—crooks his little finger and you're gone! Without a second thought—leaving me a *note*!'

'I-I didn't have any time to say any more!' Cassie stammered clumsily. 'I—'

'No time?' Joaquin practically spat the words into her pale face. 'And why was that, *querida*? Was your new lover waiting impatiently for you? Are you so insatiable that you've gone from my bed to my brother's in less than a week? Couldn't you wait to get to him—to Ramón? To *my brother*?'

'No! You've got it all wrong! I didn't—'

'Didn't what, my darling? Didn't leave me and come straight here to be with Ramón? Didn't move in with him without a backward glance—'

'Yes! I moved in with him!' she tried again. 'But not like that! We're not lovers!'

Blazing black eyes seared over her from head to foot, taking in the short, clinging robe, her bare legs and toes.

'We're *not*! When I said he gives me something you never did, I meant...'

Her voice deserted her just when she needed it most. What could she say that Ramón gave her? The mood that Joaquin was in, he would never believe her if she simply used the word friendship. And really, what Joaquin's brother had offered was more than that. It was an unquestioning, peaceful, brotherly sort of...

But no, she couldn't use the word *love*.

'What did you mean, Cassie?' Joaquin questioned
harshly, eyes cold and hard and sharp as lasers as they fixed
on her face, watching the emotions that flew across it, one
after the other, none of them actually settling. 'What does
my brother give you? What did he offer to entice you away
from me?'

'He didn't—I…'

But she couldn't finish because some change in Joaquin's
own expression alerted her to the fact that he had suddenly
had a revelation. She could see in his eyes that he had been
turning things over in his mind and had come to a conclusion—and something about the way those polished jet eyes
suddenly narrowed warned her that the assumption he had
made was not one she was going to like.

'Gives you more…' he muttered roughly. 'Something I
never did. Don't tell me the fool offered marriage!'

Cassie knew that she had lost colour. She could almost
feel the blood drain from her face so fast that it made her
already scrambled brain spin weakly.

'No—'

She tried for force but it came out as a pathetic croak,
one that she could barely hear herself, and which Joaquin,
clearly absorbed in his own thoughts, didn't even register
as he came towards her suddenly.

The look on his face frightened her. It was as if the man
she had known, her lover, the man she had lived with for
the past year, had disappeared and someone else had taken
his place. Someone she didn't know at all.

His face was hard and set, totally ruthless. There was no
longer any light in his eyes, so that they were deep, opaque,
and totally black.

Nerves dried her mouth and she took a couple of hasty
steps backwards, then had to stop as her back came up
against the wall. But Joaquin kept coming. Not fast, but his
movements measured and determined, his unyielding eyes
never even seeming to flicker or blink.

'Okay,' he said so casually that it shocked her. 'I'll bite.'

'Bite?'

She had no idea at all what he meant.

'What are you talking about?'

'Marriage.'

'M-marriage?'

She really had to be going mad. She was so stressed that she was starting to hear things. Things that were totally impossible. She could have sworn that Joaquin had said...

'Yeah, marriage.'

He pushed a hand through his hair, flexing his shoulders as if he was trying to ease some ache there, and then looked her straight in the eye.

'If marriage is what does it for you, then okay, I'll marry you.'

I'll marry you.

How many times had she dreamed of just this scenario? How many nights, tired and too weak to fight against the foolish need inside her heart, had she let herself think, let herself imagine for just the tiniest, brief moment, that one day Joaquin might ask her to marry him?

And in those dreams she had always, happily, joyfully, rushed in and said yes—yes—*yes!*—even before he had actually finished speaking.

But this time, no matter how she tried, she couldn't find the strength to speak. Three times she opened her mouth, and on each occasion her voice failed her completely. She couldn't force her tongue to form any words, felt as if her vocal cords had shrivelled into nothing, and her throat had closed up so tight that it was almost impossible to breathe.

If marriage is what does it for you, then okay, I'll marry you.

He had given her the world with one hand then snatched it back roughly with the other, reducing the gesture to less than nothing, to a lie, a mockery of any sort of real proposal. It was more like a slap in the face than any gesture of feeling.

'Well?'

'Is—is this meant to be a proposal?'

'If that's what you want it to be. What's the matter, *querida*? Not romantic enough for you?' Joaquin's tone was harder, crueller than ever—and this was the man who was suggesting marriage?

Or at least that was what it seemed.

'Would you prefer it if I went down on one knee? Sorry but I don't do that sort of romantic gesture.'

'You don't do *any* sort of romantic gesture!'

'Oh, please, *belleza*!'

Joaquin dismissed her protest with an arrogant toss of his head.

'Don't try to accuse me of short-changing you on the gestures! I gave you—what…?'

He appeared to consider, to calculate, though Cassie suspected he knew exactly what he was going to say and was only pausing for effect.

'I gave you thirteen words—two more than you spared me when you were leaving me for good. You were planning on going for good, weren't you? I mean, you didn't exactly say.'

'I…'

Cassie tried once more to answer him, and once more failed miserably. She was fighting a vicious little battle with the stinging tears at the back of her eyes; tears she was determined she would not shed. She wasn't going to let this sardonic monster that Joaquin had suddenly turned into see just how badly he was upsetting her, how deeply his barbed words had stabbed into her already wounded heart.

'Yes?' he faked concern, interest in what she had been trying to say. 'You what?'

'If—if you thought I meant to leave then why—why propose? Why ask me to marry you when you believe I wanted to go for good?'

'Because I don't want you to go.'

Don't want...

Cassie felt as if she were swimming through a dark, clouded sea, getting nowhere, or perhaps going round and round in circles. She couldn't see where she was going and so she couldn't begin to guess which way was right and which was wrong.

Had she got this all wrong? Was it possible after all that Joaquin had actually meant his proposal of marriage? That he really didn't want her to go? But if that was the case, then why had he couched it in those appalling terms? There had been no real warmth, no hint of affection or even care in those coldly casual words.

'I see it as the only way to hold onto you. You claimed you were happy with what we had—but you obviously were not. *I* was content with the way things were—'

'And that was...?'

Wasn't it obvious? the scathing glance he turned on her demanded. Did he have to explain?

Well, yes, he did, so she remained stubbornly silent until he was forced to speak again.

'We had a great thing together—the best. You know what it was like that last night.'

'The—'

Cassie's stomach heaved nauseously as she struggled with the word, forcing herself to say it.

'The sex.'

'Of course. What else, *amada*?'

His tone turned the last word into something that was exactly the opposite of the 'beloved' it actually meant.

'I wanted you from the start—and you never disappointed me. I still want you. But I want you all to myself. I'm not prepared to share you with any man—even my brother. If marriage is the price of that, then I'm prepared to pay it.'

'You'd marry me—even though you believe I've been with Ramón all this week?'

Joaquin's casually dismissive shrug was even more appallingly unfeeling than the callous way he had declared he wanted her sexually and nothing more.

'It's only a week. I can forget a momentary aberration if it's nothing more than a few days. But after this—no more! You will be mine and you will not give Ramón even a second look.'

Cassie knew that she was staring. She even suspected that her mouth was gaping slightly in stunned horror, but she couldn't shake herself out of the almost catatonic state into which his cold-blooded declaration had thrown her.

He couldn't mean this! He just *couldn't*!

He had to be joking—but then, if he was, it was the most dreadful, sick form of black humour imaginable. It was vicious and cruel and totally hateful.

'So what's your answer?'

'My answer!'

Pushed beyond endurance, Cassie felt that her head might explode. But at least his taunting tone drove the tears away, drying them in an instant. She welcomed the tiny flame of rage that lit inside her, fanning it until it flared into a healthy blaze.

'What do you think my answer is? What would any sane woman answer to such a travesty of a proposal? I don't know how you even dare to think I might have to consider it.'

Wasn't that enough for him to get the message? But looking into the bleak darkness of his eyes she saw that no, it wasn't. He was actually waiting for her response. Waiting for her to say something more—to give him an answer to his hateful suggestion.

'My answer is no! *No!* Never! No way! Not in my lifetime! I wouldn't marry you if you were the last man alive on this earth and the future of the human race depended on it.'

Drawing a deep breath, she locked her blazing blue gaze with his cold jet one and repeated, with insulting slowness and clarity, 'My answer is no—I will not marry you!'

In the deathly silence that fell as her words died away she tensed instinctively, waiting for the explosion that she was sure was to come. An explosion of anger, or protest, or rejection—she wasn't sure which. But she was positive that there was no way at all that he was just going to take that and leave it, without coming back at her in some way.

So she was stunned when once again he just shrugged his shoulders in nonchalant dismissal.

'Fine. Okay, if that's your answer.'

'It is.'

She sounded as breathless as if she had been running for hours, the words escaping on shaken gasps.

'Believe me—it is.'

'Well, in that case, then, I won't stay around.' His tone was as stiff as the muscles in his neck and jaw, drawing his mouth tight and hard. 'I'm sure—just from looking at you—that you're expecting my brother any moment now, and it would probably be best if I wasn't here when he arrived. *Buenas noches*, Cassie.'

This time Cassie knew she was really gaping, but she couldn't stop herself. She just didn't believe what she was seeing as he turned on his heel and marched towards the door.

'Joaquin...' she managed, not really knowing what she meant to say.

But her voice had no strength and Joaquin didn't hear her. Or if he did he ignored her and kept on walking, his head arrogantly high, the broad shoulders and stiff, straight back expressing eloquently his total rejection of her without a word needing to be spoken.

He didn't look back either, but then she had never expected that he would. And she couldn't move, the after-effects of shock and the wild emotional storm that had raged through her leaving her shaken and weak, unable even to think.

She let him go. Let him walk through the door, and watched it slam closed behind him, the terrible, unfocused, dreary sense of inevitability swamping her mind so that there was no room for anything else.

It was a dreadfully bitter irony that now, at last, Joaquin had done what she had wanted most in all the world. He had told her that he wanted her; that he didn't want to lose her. He had even proposed *marriage*, for heaven's sake!

But it hadn't been for heaven, had it? Instead it had produced Cassie's own personal form of hell. A hell in which by apparently offering her everything she had ever wanted, a future with him, he had shown that the real truth of the way he was feeling was the exact opposite of what she truly needed.

He wanted her. He didn't want to lose her. He thought of her as 'his woman'—but he didn't love her. He would marry her, but only as a way of possessing her. The offer of marriage had been only to ensure that she had no relationship with his brother.

His brother!

'Ramón!' Cassie muttered aloud, the name bringing her out of the trancelike shock and into action again.

Joaquin still believed that she was having a relationship with his brother! He thought that he had left her here awaiting the arrival of her lover—of Ramón!

She couldn't let that continue; couldn't let him go on believing that his brother had made a move on 'his woman' while, ostensibly at least, Joaquin and Cassie had still been together. It was the sort of thing that Joaquin's pride could never tolerate. The sort of thing that no man with any sense of honour would do to a friend, let alone a member of his own family.

Joaquin would never speak to his brother again if he continued to believe that was what had happened. And Cassie could not be the cause of anger and division between the two brothers. She knew that they had had a difficult enough time getting to be friends in the past. Joaquin had seen his half-brother as evidence of their father's adultery, his unfaithfulness to his wife, and so had had to struggle to accept both the younger man and then the other, half-English brother Alex who had appeared later. She had to make sure that Joaquin knew the truth. She couldn't live with herself if she didn't at least try.

'Joaquin!'

Heedless of the fact that she was still wearing only the flimsy robe and that her feet were bare, Cassie yanked open the door and ran out into the big hallway, the third floor landing in the apartment block.

'Joaquin!'

Her call echoed round the empty space. Of course. The mood he had been in, Joaquin was clearly in no frame of mind to hang around. But somewhere in the distance, a floor or so away, she caught the faint sound of footsteps on the stairs, going down. Perhaps if she ran, she might just have a chance to catch him.

Bare feet making no sound, her hand clutching the polished wooden banister rail as she swung round the corners, she dashed down the big staircase, her breath catching in her throat at the thought that he might get away before she could speak to him.

'Joaquin, please wait!'

Had the footsteps below her slowed, maybe even stilled, just for a second? She didn't know and she couldn't risk a pause to listen for fear that he might get right away from her. If he went out into the street she would lose him...

'Oh, please!'

She landed on the marble tiled floor of the main entrance hall with a soft thud, her heart lifting jerkily at the realisation that she could just see Joaquin's tall, dark figure on the other side of the glass-paned door that was still swinging with the force of his exit through it.

'*Joaquin!*'

Somehow she found the strength to wrench it open, fling herself out into the evening air where a sudden rainstorm had soaked the street, the shallow stone steps leading up to the apartment building.

'Joaquin, oh, please! Please wait! Please listen! I *have* to talk to you.'

He'd heard her.

She saw him stiffen, hesitate, then whirl round, spinning on his heel.

And as he did so it seemed as if time suddenly slowed, went out of focus and blurred. Even her own breathing suddenly seemed suspended and she watched in a sense of hopeless horror as the scene before her was played out in a sort of dreadful slow motion that she could do nothing to stop.

She saw Joaquin's swift stride down the steps, the way his foot had gone out to move from one to the next. Then his check as she called his name. The swift, sudden turn, his head coming round to glance at her, that threw him totally off balance. The way that, still moving forward at the same time, he missed his footing, slipped, lost his balance completely.

She thought that she screamed. She knew that she opened her mouth to do so, but no sound came out.

And she could only watch in silent dread as Joaquin pitched forward, fell headlong down the remainder of the steps, landing awkwardly on the rain-soaked pavement below.

Fear froze her with her hands to her mouth as she saw his dark head strike hard against the hard stone of the final step, his long body rolling a couple of inches more then coming to a complete halt, lying dreadfully limp and unmoving on the pavement while the heavy rain lashed down onto his pale, still face.

CHAPTER SIX

A MAN like Joaquin didn't belong in a hospital bed.

He was too big, too strong, too forceful, too vibrant, too *alive* to be contained in such a small space. And lying there, silent and still, unnervingly pale in spite of his tan, he looked shockingly reduced, younger, and infinitely more vulnerable.

Cassie didn't know how many times this particular thought had crossed her mind throughout this, the longest night of her life. She only knew that it was the one she most often came back to, unhappy and unwilling, wishing there were something—anything she could do to ease the situation.

But Joaquin just lay there, unconscious and unmoving, his handsome face disfigured by the ugly bruise that had spread across his forehead, marking the spot where his skull had collided with the hard stone of the steps.

And Cassie sat by his bed, holding his limp hand and willing him to wake up, open his eyes.

'Joaquin, can you hear me? Please show me that you can!' she pleaded with him. 'Please—just open your eyes—show me you're all right. Please!'

She couldn't believe the way that the world she thought she knew had turned to a waking nightmare. One minute she had been running down the stairs calling to Joaquin to stop, to wait—the next she had found herself crouched in the lashing rain beside his unconscious form, heedless of the way that the downpour had soaked into the thin silk of her skimpy robe, moulding it wetly to her body.

She had screamed at the hovering security guard to call an ambulance, tried to protect Joaquin's face from the appalling weather, and waited for what seemed like an age for help to arrive. All the time she had held his hand, stroking it softly, telling him that everything was going to be all right—that he was going to be fine.

It had been there that Ramón had found her. Arriving home at last, he had taken in the situation in a glance, and immediately taken charge. After that things had happened fast. The ambulance had arrived; Joaquin had been lifted gently into it and they had set off for the hospital. Cassie had wanted to go with them, and only Ramón's gentle logic had persuaded her otherwise.

'You're soaked through, sweetheart,' he told her. 'You'll make yourself ill if you don't get changed out of that wet robe. Believe me, Joaquin's in good hands—and you'll be much better able to help if you're dry and comfortable. This could be a long night.'

And he was right.

Cassie dried herself off and dressed in a navy shirt and jeans as quickly as she could, throwing a white cotton cardigan over her shoulders as protection against the chill that the rain had brought to the night air, and pushing her bare feet into lightweight slip-on shoes. Before Ramón had time to down the coffee he'd made for himself, she was ready to go, anxious to reach the hospital as soon as possible.

But after that things slowed down again. Once they reached the hospital it was to find that nothing very much happened fast. There were what seemed to Cassie like endless long hours spent waiting, with very little news to tell at the end of them.

As far as the doctors could tell, Joaquin hadn't sustained any major injury. There was no fracture, nothing to worry about there. But he had had a nasty blow to his head, and he was deeply unconscious. They would monitor the situation overnight and watch what happened.

So Cassie settled in for the long vigil through the dark hours of the night. She settled in a chair beside the bed, took hold of Joaquin's hand, fixed her eyes on his face, and waited...

She wasn't alone. From the start, Ramón had stayed with her, and later, after he had phoned his brother's family, Joaquin's father and his younger sister Mercedes arrived in the small private room too.

The other brother, Alex, they discovered, was already at the hospital for his own reasons. His wife, Louise, who was expecting their first child, had gone into labour earlier that evening and he was in the maternity ward with her. He was obviously torn between two loyalties until Cassie took pity on him.

'You should be with Louise,' she told him. 'She needs you. And everyone's sure that Joaquin's going to be all right. There's no need for all of us to stay here. If anything happens, Ramón and I will let you know.'

If the truth was told, she much preferred being on her own, or with just the silent, watchful Ramón for company. The doctors had told her that it could do some good to keep talking to Joaquin, that he might be able to hear her and the sound of her voice might bring him out of the coma he had fallen into.

After the long, lonely week of being separated from him she welcomed the chance to be able to speak to him at last. And because of the darkness and the stillness of the night, because Joaquin's eyes were closed and she didn't have to face his reaction to anything she said, she snatched at the chance to tell him the truth about how she felt, murmuring to him how much she cared for him, telling him that he was her love, her life, her reason for existing. All the things that she would never dare to tell him to his face, because she was afraid of seeing the way his expression would change, the cynical scorn that would darken his strongly carved features.

She didn't know whether she prayed that he could hear her or hoped devoutly that he did not. All she knew was that for once and perhaps for the only time in her life she had her chance to tell the man she loved just how she felt about him, and she couldn't let that go without taking full advantage of it.

But telling Joaquin of her love reminded her of the brutal marriage proposal he had made to her earlier that evening, the grim travesty of a declaration of feeling that had accompanied it. And in her mind she heard again his voice declaring: 'I want you all to myself. I'm not prepared to share you with any man—even my brother.'

'Ramón,' she said hastily, turning to where he sat in the corner, 'there's something I have to tell you.'

'Can't it wait?' Joaquin's brother asked. 'It's late—we're both tired…'

'It's important!'

She couldn't leave Ramón in the dark about what had happened between her and Joaquin earlier that evening. She had to let him know about the suspicions his brother had had, the faulty conclusion he had jumped to about their relationship. If she left it unsaid, and Joaquin came round to find his brother here, with her, then she shuddered to think of the possible repercussions that might follow. Recalling Joaquin's rage, his savage bitterness, she couldn't let his brother face that unprepared.

'Okay.'

Cassie drew a breath, wondering where to start.

'If it helps, I think I know what this is about,' Ramón put in. 'You were lying when you said you and Joaquin had come to the end of the line. *He* might have, but there's no way that you—'

He broke off, staring hard at his unconscious brother.

'Did he just…?'

'I didn't hear anything,' Cassie began.

But at that moment a faint sound from the bed brought her head swinging round. Joaquin's eyelids were fluttering, lifting slightly, half opening, then falling closed again as he gave a heavy, tired sigh.

'Joaquin!'

At once all her attention was focused on him, her hand reaching for and clasping his fingers tight.

'Joaquin, can you hear me? Are you okay?'

Another sigh was his only response. His eyes remained tightly closed.

But then he stirred again, moving his head slightly on the crisp white pillows. Clearly the movement disturbed him because he frowned faintly, made a small murmur of protest.

'Joaquin?' Cassie tried again.

Joaquin, darling, she wanted to say. Joaquin, my love, wake up! Let me see that you're all right…

But she didn't dare.

Remembering how she and Joaquin had parted—the blunt, outright rejection of his mockery of a proposal; the way that he had stormed from Ramón's apartment—she had little doubt that he would rebuff any attempt on her part to show him the way she really felt. So she had to content herself with simply repeating his name, trying to draw him out of his dazed, half-conscious state into more awareness.

'Joaquin? Can you hear me?'

This time she got a definite response. The heavy eyelids lifted slowly again and his dark, dark eyes looked straight into her anxious blue ones. But Joaquin's gaze was clouded with confusion and lack of focus and when he frowned again in bewilderment she knew that he was only conscious, but still not thinking straight.

'Where…?' he managed and his voice croaked so badly, it was clearly such an effort to speak, that it tore at Cassie's already far too sensitive heart just to hear it.

She was so used to knowing the Joaquin who was always totally strong, totally composed, totally in control, that to

see him like this, struggling even to focus, was almost more
than she could bear.

'You're in hospital. You had a fall—and hit your head.
Do you remember?'

'No...'

Again it was just a sigh and his hand went up to touch
the spot on his forehead where the bruising was worst,
flinching away swiftly at even the faintest pressure on a
tender point.

'Careful!'

Cassie moved instinctively to lift his hand, then hesitated, her teeth worrying at her lower lip at the thought that
she didn't know how he would react. She couldn't take it
if he pulled away from her, or rejected her in some other,
more forceful way.

'That's where you hit your head,' she said, schooling her
voice into neutrality with an effort. 'It's bound to be a bit
sore.'

Was she imagining things or did Joaquin's mouth twitch
into a faint, ironic smile at the deliberate understatement?
He seemed to be coming round fast and that was something
that filled her with painfully ambiguous feelings. She
wanted him to wake properly, needed desperately to see
that he was all right and was well on the road to recovery,
but a nasty little worm of fear was eating at her heart at
the thought of what that would mean.

She would lose this quiet, peaceful time with him. It
would become just the lull between two storms. When he
woke fully and recalled the scene in Ramón's apartment,
she wouldn't be able to sit here, beside his bed, holding
his hand. He wouldn't want her close to him. In fact he
probably wouldn't even let her stay in the room at all. If
she knew Joaquin, he would order her out of his presence
at once—and he would fully expect to be obeyed.

'Just relax,' she said cautiously. 'Don't try to fight
things.'

His eyes were opening again, a little more easily, more definitely this time. His black gaze was better focused too, which made her heart give a little kick of excitement at the way he was improving.

The next moment, that excitement grew into a real glow of delight. Joaquin managed to open his eyes fully, shifting his head slightly on the pillows again, and looking straight at her.

And he smiled.

It was a little vague, a little lopsided, but it was directed solely at her. The anger and rejection she had expected wasn't there. Instead, Joaquin smiled straight at her.

'Hi,' she said softly.

'I'd better tell the nurses he's come round.' It was Ramón's voice, coming from directly behind her. 'And Papá and Mercedes will want to know too.'

'Mmm.'

The strangled sound that might have been one of agreement was all that Cassie could manage. She felt as if she had just been slapped in the face with a very cold and slimy, nasty-smelling cloth.

Had that smile, from which she had taken such pleasure, and such comfort, not been meant for her? Ramón had been standing just behind her at that moment, directly in Joaquin's line of sight.

So had he in fact been smiling, not at her, but at his *brother*?

The rush of joy fled swiftly, dissipating like air from a pricked balloon, and leaving her as limp and deflated as the flat piece of coloured rubber that was all that would be left behind.

Joaquin's eyes had drifted shut again. Perhaps he was asleep. Perhaps he had slipped into unconsciousness again. She shouldn't disturb him, but the unanswered question was nagging at her brain, fretting in her heart.

She *had* to know the answer!

Had Joaquin meant that smile for her? If he woke again, properly this time, would he welcome her presence at his side as he had seemed to do a moment ago? Or had she been totally mistaken, and he had in fact been looking at Ramón? Would the anger and the bitterness of the time in his brother's apartment resurface? Or had he actually decided to forgive her?

'Joaquin?' she tried again softly. 'Joaquin, are you awake?'

'Tired...'

His response was a vaguely formed murmur, but at least he had heard her, was still listening.

'Shall—?' She had to force herself to ask the question. 'Shall I go?'

The jet-black brows twitched together sharply in a frown, his eyes still staying closed. Apart from that one tiny reaction, he didn't speak, but lay silent and still as before.

The bubble of hope that had formed inside Cassie's heart disintegrated in a rush. Perhaps that smile *had* been for Ramón.

'Shall I go?'

Still no answer.

She studied Joaquin's still face, seeing the way that the long, lush black lashes lay fanned out above the high slanting cheekbones, illuminated by the light from a lamp at the side of the bed. The ebony sheen of his hair was stark against the crisp white of the pillowcases, his skin looking a darker bronze.

Her gaze was drawn to the beautifully sensual shape of his mouth. The need to lean forward and press her own lips to that mouth was like a hard kick in her guts, one she had to fight so hard to resist. But she was relieved to see that his features were more relaxed, the total unconsciousness of earlier, outside the apartment building, easing away.

Seen like this, with the jet-hard darkness of his eyes hidden behind the closed lids, he looked younger, gentler, less

dangerous somehow. Even though she knew she was probably deceiving herself, Cassie was tempted to let herself
believe that this Joaquin, this quiet, peaceful man, would
have smiled at her. That he would be able to accept that
she wasn't living with Ramón in the way that he had orig-
inally believed, and that maybe—maybe they could have
more?

But that was just a dream, and she knew it. If he opened
his eyes then she was afraid that all would change. She
would see the cold light in those deep dark eyes, his face
would resume its hard, aloof expression, and she would
know her present mood for the fantasy that it was.

'I'll leave you to rest,' she murmured, reluctantly loosening her grip on his fingers.

But as she slowly eased away a sudden movement of
Joaquin's hand startled her into stillness once more.

'No!'

Still with his eyes closed, he reached out and grabbed at
her fingers, closing his around them, firm and tight. And as
Cassie gasped in sudden shock he forced his heavy eyelids
open again, looking straight into her face.

'No!' he said again, more forcefully this time.

'What is it?'

Try as she might, she couldn't erase the tremor from her
voice. Was this the time when he remembered? When everything became clear to him again? She fought to contain
the panic that was rising up inside her, struggled to ensure
that the hand he held didn't shake in his grasp.

'Cassandra—queda, por favor…'

He was tiring even as he spoke. She could see the blurring of his gaze, sense the loosening of his focus as his
eyelids drooped again.

'Queda…'

His grip on her hand loosened as he drifted into sleep.
But Cassie didn't need any restraining grip to hold her
there. If the hospital had been on fire, the room filling with

smoke, she would have stayed right where she was, as long as Joaquin was there. Nothing would have forced her to move, unless he went with her.

Queda, he had said.

Stay.

And he had added *por favor*.

Queda, por favor...Stay—*please*!

Her heart felt as if it would burst with happiness, in a way that was such a stunning contrast to the fear and apprehension with which she had begun the evening that it made her head swim in sheer delight.

Stay. Joaquin had said. Stay—please. He wanted her with him, didn't want her to go. And that was all she needed, holding as it did the promise of so much more. Of reconciliation and a hope for the future that she had thought she had lost for good.

Even though she knew that Joaquin was asleep, or very nearly so, and that he wouldn't hear her, she knew she had to answer him out loud, the words too important to keep to herself.

'Of course I'll stay,' she said in a voice that was thick and rough with emotion. 'For as long as you want—as long as you need me.'

And now, at last, she could no longer find the strength to hold back her tears but simply let them fall, cascading down her cheeks in a show of open emotion. But this time she didn't care, because these tears were tears of happiness, the outward expression of the joy she felt inside.

Joaquin had spent an uncomfortable couple of days in which he hadn't known quite what was real, and what was part of the weird, heightened dreams that had haunted the sleep into which he fell with a disturbing regularity. They were so vivid, so confusing, that he would have described them as delirium, even though he had been assured that he was not running a temperature.

People came and went and he never quite knew when or why. Sometimes he would open his eyes and his father was there, or Ramón, and then another time it would be Mercedes who was sitting in the chair by the bed—and occasionally Alex. He seemed to recall that Alex had said something about a baby, but it had blurred into the haze in his head and he couldn't recall any details.

Sometimes it would be bright day, with the warm sunshine pouring in through the windows; at other times, clearly night had fallen without him noticing and the world beyond the glass was dark, the room lit softly by the bedside lamp. He'd eaten sometimes, just a bit, not tasting anything, and he'd drunk the water people kept offering him and found that that tasted surprisingly good.

But every time his eyes opened, it was always Cassandra that he saw. Day or night. Early or late. She was there. Sitting by the bed, or on the bed. Silent and watchful or talking about something that he couldn't always take in. She was a calm, reassuring presence in a world that seemed to be always out of focus. And she was *always* there.

That was fine with him.

More than fine.

He knew that he had spoken to the other visitors, murmuring something that they had seemed to accept as the answer to whatever they had asked, but he couldn't really recall just what he had said. The one thing he actually registered, the one thing he remembered saying, was that he had asked Cassandra to stay.

He had asked her to stay, and she had stayed.

And that was fine too.

In the end, after three hazy days, the fog that had clouded his brain finally started to clear. He no longer drifted asleep at totally unexpected moments, his eyes focused much better, and he could actually understand what people were saying to him. To his intense relief, he was also let out of the damn bed, and felt decidedly more human once he was sitting in a chair, wearing proper clothes and with his jaw shaved free of the impossibly luxuriant growth of beard that had resulted from three days' lack of attention.

He would feel even better if the doctors would only let him go home.

If he went home, then he could be alone with Cassandra.

But: 'You have had a very nasty knock on the head,' they said. 'We need to be sure that there's no permanent damage. What can you remember about the accident itself?'

'Remember? The honest answer is not a damn thing— but that's not so unusual, is it? I understand that quite often in an accident where someone is knocked unconscious, they can't remember the actual event. The bang on the head sends it out of your mind.'

'Yes, that can often be the case.'

'I understand I was at my brother's apartment. That I slipped on the steps outside, fell, hit my head. Luckily, my girlfriend was with me…what is it?'

He had caught the look that had passed between the two doctors. A slightly concerned, slightly questioning look. One he didn't like at all. One that worried him.

'What is it?' he repeated. 'What the hell's wrong now?'

'Nothing to concern yourself about,' they assured him. 'But we would like to ask you just a few more questions.'

'Okay,' Joaquin growled impatiently. 'Ask. Anything, if it will help me get out of this damn place.'

So they asked and he answered. And their reaction to his responses turned his thoughts inside out and made his head reel in shock.

CHAPTER SEVEN

'THE doctor says *what*?'

It was Mercedes who asked the question, the surprise and shock they were all feeling ringing in her voice. And Cassandra could only be grateful that Joaquin's younger sister had no hesitation in responding so fast and so forcefully to what her brother had just told them. At least it hid the way that she was unable to speak herself, her silence the result of a sense of shock that had made her thoughts reel.

'He says that I have partial amnesia,' Joaquin explained with an exaggerated patience that made it plain that he didn't want to have to go through all the details yet again, even if his family needed to hear them. 'It's not just the immediate events of the accident that I can't remember— there's quite a bit more that's been wiped too.'

'How much?' Cassie forced herself to ask it, then immediately wished she hadn't as her voice was such a revealingly painful croak that she felt hot colour flood her cheeks in embarrassment at the sound.

'Weeks.' Joaquin's tone was wry. 'The last thing I can remember with any clarity is Mercedes' birthday party.'

'But that's almost a month ago!' his sister exclaimed.

Almost a month ago, and perhaps the last time they had been truly happy together, Cassie admitted to herself. She and Joaquin had had a wonderful time at that party, dancing together under the stars, and then they had gone back home and held a long, passionate party all of their own. Spending the rest of the night in bed, but definitely not sleeping.

It was after that that things had started to go wrong. When Cassie had started to worry about the dates on the calendar, and the significance of their upcoming anniversary—the importance of Joaquin's uncompromising one-year rule.

But if all that Joaquin remembered was the night of the party then it was no wonder that he had smiled at her as he'd come round. No wonder that he had begged her to stay.

He had forgotten all that had happened in between, the rows, the anxieties, the way that he had declared so openly to her face that he 'didn't do' commitment. The images of the appalling night at Ramón's apartment, when he had come hunting for her and, finding her there, had leapt to the conclusion that she and his brother were lovers, had been wiped from his brain by the blow to the head he had suffered after storming out of the building and falling on the stone steps.

So he hadn't forgiven her at all. Hadn't rethought the whole situation and realised his mistake and resolved to put things right. The smile that he had given her—the smile that had meant so much to her—had been meant in a way for a totally different person. And the woman he had asked to stay with him was not the one he really remembered at all, but an echo of a month ago, before everything had changed.

'So—' Her voice cracked hoarsely and she had to slick her tongue over her dry lips in order to moisten them, swallowing hard before she could go on. 'So you remember nothing about the accident—about that night.'

'Not a thing.'

Frowning darkly, Joaquin raked both his hands through his hair in a gesture that revealed the unsettled state of his thoughts much better than any words.

'*Nada*. I don't even know what I—we—were doing at Ramón's. Why were we there?'

'Why…?'

Why were we there? Cassie's thoughts spun in panic as

she struggled to think of some way to answer him. But what could she say that wouldn't reveal the truth? How could she explain that she had been living with Ramón without arousing once again the savage, furious jealousy that had sent Joaquin raging out of the apartment and into the rain that night?

'I—you…'

'The doctors say we mustn't tell you anything.'

It was Ramón's voice that cut in sharply. He had been standing outside in the corridor, talking to the specialist who had been treating Joaquin, and luckily he came into the room just at this moment.

'Nothing at all,' he went on, after one swift, warning glance into Cassie's troubled face. 'They say that we mustn't push anything or try to make you remember. That we have to leave it all to come back in its own time. Or not at all.'

'And what if it *is* not at all?' Joaquin growled, obviously not happy about this.

'Then we'll deal with that when it comes to it,' his brother assured him breezily. 'But they seem pretty certain that it won't. A thump on the head like the one you suffered was bound to scramble your brains just a bit. You need to take things steady, wait for everything to settle back down again. And not get in a mood about things or you could face a setback.'

'I'm not a baby.' Joaquin scowled. Cassie could guess at the sort of thoughts that were going through his head. An unfailingly strong and healthy man, he had clearly been shaken by finding himself in hospital, and he obviously hated the restrictions that his accident had placed on him, even if for just a few days.

'Give it time,' she said, trying to soothe him. 'It's only been a couple of days so far. Who knows what difference a week might make?'

Who knows? Cassie echoed to herself, not knowing whether it was something she should hope for or dread.

How was she supposed to act with Joaquin now? He might not remember all that had happened in that missing month—but she couldn't *forget* a thing. He thought that they were still happy together, that nothing had come between them. He certainly didn't suspect her of having an affair with his half-brother—at least not now!

But what would happen when he did remember? When he realised that that smile, that 'Stay', had been directed at that other Cassie, the one who no longer existed in his buried memories and heart.

She might have a reprieve now. A chance to go back to how it had once been. A chance to live once more in harmony and happiness with Joaquin, but there was no way it could last. Some time, inevitably, Joaquin's thoughts would clear, and he would remember everything and then they would be right back where they had been on that dreadful night in the moments before he had had his accident.

'All right,' Joaquin conceded unwillingly. 'If that's what the doctors advise, then I suppose I'll have to go along with it. Anything, so long as they let me out of this place. And they've said I can go home.'

'But only if you have someone who will look after you,' Cassie put in unthinkingly, wishing she'd bitten her tongue when she saw Joaquin's look of surprise.

'Well, of course I'll have someone to look after me. I'll have you.'

'I—'

Cassie caught Ramón's warning glance, and hastily adjusted what she had been about to say.

'Of course,' she managed uneasily, thinking of the isolation of the big house in the country, of herself and Joaquin alone there together through the long days...the nights.

'You could both come home to us if you'd prefer,'

Mercedes put in. 'I'm sure Papá would be delighted to have you there, and your room is empty.'

Cassie glanced automatically at Joaquin's face, seeing the determined 'No way!' expression that was stamped onto his hard features. But perhaps it might not be such a bad idea. There would be plenty of other people around to distract Joaquin, Mercedes and his father to talk to…

But then she hastily rethought.

On the few occasions they had visited Joaquin's father and sister in the past, Juan Alcolar had proved remarkably and unexpectedly tolerant about the fact that she and his son were a couple. They had always been given a room together, always the same one. And so now she knew only too well that that was the room Mercedes was referring to as 'your room'.

In his father's house they would automatically be expected to share a bedroom—and a bed. And that was something she didn't feel at all happy about right now.

Happy? The thought had all the nerves in her stomach tying themselves in knots.

At the *finca*, there was at least plenty of space—lots of bedrooms. She could make up some excuse—she'd *have* to—she couldn't tell Joaquin why she wouldn't share his bed.

'We'll go home,' she said, praying that the terrible, hollow feeling in the pit of her stomach hadn't been echoed in the sound of her voice.

Obviously not, because Joaquin's wide, brilliant grin, missing from his face for so long, resurfaced at her words and she was bathed in its warmth. For a moment she gloried in the sensation, but then a double whammy of realisation hit her hard in the stomach, driving all the air from her body in a faint gasp of horror.

'Is something wrong?'

Joaquin had caught the sound, sparking his curiosity.

'N-no—it's just that I—I remembered…'

'Remembered what?'

Cassie's mind went blank with panic. How could she say that she had just remembered how long it had in fact been since she had seen that smile on Joaquin's face? Almost as far back as the night of Mercedes' party, which was the point at which Joaquin's memories stopped. It was after that that he had started drifting away from her, losing the warm closeness they had shared and becoming colder, more distant with each day that had passed. Coupled with that had come the realisation of how little Joaquin actually meant that smile, did he but know it. When his memory returned, then all the warmth of it would fade from his face, his handsome features setting taut into a cold animosity, his eyes taking on the gleam of polished jet, opaque and totally impenetrable.

'I remembered…'

'That you have some things you'll need to collect from my place before you head home,' Ramón put in quietly, subtly reminding her that all her clothes, everything she had taken with her when she'd left his house, were still in the guest bedroom in his apartment.

'Oh—yes.'

Cassie flashed him a grateful look. She was no good at this sort of deception, no good at all. That was why she had had to leave the *finca* when Joaquin had made his feelings for her so plain. She could not have lived with him and not given away the state of her own emotions. It had been strained enough in the last couple of weeks; she couldn't go through that again.

'I have to go and pick them up.'

And do it without Joaquin finding out. How was she going to manage this?

'We can do it on the way home,' Joaquin stated firmly.

Which was just the sort of thing she was most dreading.

'And go all the way back into town and then out again? It would add almost half an hour to the trip.'

'I'll drive Joaquin home.'

Once more Ramón came to her rescue.

'I have my car here after all, and it's bigger and more comfortable than yours—you'd have a much easier ride,' he added with enviable casualness to his brother. 'Then Cassie can go to my flat, pick up her bits and come along in her own car. Here, Cassie...'

He tossed her his house key, which she caught neatly and headed for the door before Joaquin could voice the protest that was clearly hovering on his lips.

'I'll see you there,' she tossed over her shoulder, escaping thankfully from the tension that had been clawing at her ever since she had first heard the news about the lingering after-effects of the blow to Joaquin's head.

As she hurried down the hospital corridor, the keys clutched so tightly in her hand that later she would find the impression of them embedded in her flesh, she found that her heart was thudding hard, sending the blood racing round her body in a flurry of panic that she could no longer subdue.

Just how was she going to get through the next couple of days—maybe even the next couple of weeks, if it took that long? She couldn't lie to Joaquin for all that time, but then, at the same time, she had been forbidden to tell him the truth.

He had to remember for himself, the doctors had insisted—no good would come of trying to force things. The possible consequences of that could be risky, even dangerous. And for a week or so at least, Joaquin had to avoid any stress, any upset that might cause a relapse, or worse.

So for the time it took for the memories he had lost to return, Cassie had to live with him and pretend that nothing was wrong. She would have to act as if they had never rowed, never split up, never...

With a soft moan, she stopped dead, leaned back against the wall and covered her face with her hands, struggling for control. She had to pretend that all was well, while all the time knowing that as soon as Joaquin discovered the truth—or what he believed to be the truth—he would see this time she spent with him as one of deliberate deception, perhaps even trying to win him round by concealing the truth.

She had no way out. She was damned if she did, damned if she didn't. She had never really understood the phrase about being caught in a cleft stick before, but she did now. She could not go forward, and she could not go back. She could only stay where she was, marking time, and knowing that one day, with a dreadful inevitability, the truth would all come out.

CHAPTER EIGHT

'I THOUGHT we would never get here!'

Joaquin's impatient stride into the house matched the irritation in his tone.

'When did you become such an old woman when you drive?'

'I was taking care of you,' his brother pointed out reasonably, his soothing tone grating on Joaquin's already badly rattled nerves. 'You've just had a—'

'A nasty accident—I know, I know!' Joaquin snapped. 'But I'm not an invalid. I don't need wrapping in cotton wool!'

He pushed his hands into the pockets of the black jeans that Cassandra had brought to the hospital that morning, shoulders hunched under the white polo shirt, and glared at his brother. Ramón appeared totally unconcerned by his irritation.

'And *I* don't want to be responsible for you suffering any sort of setback.'

'Oh, I don't think there's much likelihood of that! Unless you count the possibilities of exhaustion from the length of time it took to get here. Cassandra would have had time to get to your place, collect whatever it was that she'd left there and *still* get here before us.'

If she was here at all, some nasty little voice inserted into his brain. Deep down, he knew that this was the real reason for his irritation and that he was taking it out on Ramón quite unnecessarily.

His real anxieties centred around Cassandra, and the problem was that he had no idea why. But he had seen the look on her face when he had said that he wanted to come home, and she had fled from the hospital room looking as if all the hounds in hell were after her. All he could imagine was that they must have had some sort of a major row in the time he couldn't remember.

That was something he was determined to get to the bottom of. But first he had to get rid of Ramón. Only when he and Cassandra were alone together could he start to find out anything that mattered.

A sound from upstairs caught his attention, had him moving to the foot of the stairs.

'Cassandra! Is that you?' he called, then frowned as something swirled inside his head.

It was just a hint. Just a momentary flash on the screen of his mind. A feeling that he had done this before.

But then, of course, that was inevitable. This was his home. He must have done this or something similar dozens—more—times over the time he and Cassandra had been together. It was nothing.

'I'm here.'

She had appeared at the top of the stairs while his mind was distracted, and now she started down towards him, a welcoming smile on her face.

'I was just making up the bed—putting fresh sheets on it. Yes—I know!'

She had caught his expression and interpreted it with unnerving accuracy.

'You don't want to have to lie down—and you don't have to, so long as you take things easy. But I wanted things ready. Then if you do feel tired…'

A swift glance at his face had her trailing the words off.

'All right, I won't fuss. But you must take things steady. It's so good to see you back here.'

Moving up close, she gave him a swift, firm hug. But when his arms would have closed around her, holding her tight, enveloping her in the sort of hug that had been impossible while he was stuck in the hospital bed, she seemed to almost slip out of his grasp like water through his fingers, drifting away again, out of reach before he had even had a chance to be aware that she'd moved.

'I've missed you,' she said.

Amen to that! was the thought that echoed inside Joaquin's head. That hug, the contact, brief though it had been, had brought home to him just how much he had missed her.

Just to touch her, to feel the warmth and softness of her body in his arms, to inhale her scent, the mixture of some herbal shampoo on her hair, the light, tangy perfume that she wore, was enough to switch his senses into overdrive. But it was the deeper, more intensely personal, faintly musky aroma of her skin that kicked him deep in the gut, hardening him in an instant, setting off the sort of hot, clamouring demand that had him gritting his teeth against a betraying groan.

He wanted her so badly. He felt as if he had been starved of her for weeks, not just the couple of days he had been in the hospital.

If his brother hadn't been here then he would never have let her go. Even as she slipped away, he would have grabbed her, hauled her hard up against him, pulled her face up to meet his own and taken her mouth with all the force of the hunger he was feeling. Kissing her until they were both out of their minds with need.

But Ramón was here, damn him. And so he had to smile and say as calmly as he could that he had missed her too. And yes, coffee would be nice. He was parched, could kill for a drink.

What he could really kill for was *not* coffee.

If he couldn't have Cassandra, in his bed, naked underneath him, right now—then a glass of the finest *crianza* might come a reasonable second. But he could just see Cassandra's frown if he suggested that. Not yet, she would say. You're supposed to be taking things steady.

He would erupt if one more person told him to take things steady.

Oh, he knew why, of course. He understood. He even saw the sense in it—if he had to. But the trouble was that he didn't *feel* steady, or sensible, or even calm, though he supposed he must look it on the surface to both his brother and his woman. Long experience of discussing business terms, negotiating deals, had taught him how to wear a controlled, affable mask when he needed to conceal his real feelings. But what he felt was a different matter.

What he felt right now was like a ticking bomb. He had lost a month out of his life in the blink of an eye and everyone seemed to expect him to just accept it, go with the flow, until things came back to him.

If they ever came back to him.

But everyone else knew what had happened in that month, while he'd had it wiped from his mind. He'd lived through four weeks that he didn't remember and those four weeks...

Those four weeks—what? Hell, he didn't know! He couldn't even begin to guess. But if the way that Cassandra was behaving was anything to go by, then something had happened in that time. Because she sure as damnation wasn't the same with him as the Cassandra he remembered.

That Cassandra hadn't been edgy with him, elusive, impossible to pin down. She wouldn't have come into his arms and then dodged out of them, flighty as a butterfly. And she hadn't had those shadows in her eyes, the ones that lurked at the back of this woman's eyes. The ones that darkened and clouded the bright blue of her gaze and made him feel that there was something he just didn't understand.

And even that could be wrong.

Damn it, he didn't know anything. He could be jumping to conclusions, imagining things. And the worst thing was that he couldn't even *ask*! If he did, then no one would tell him because he was supposed to wait for it all to come back to him.

Wait for *what* to come back to him?

'Joaquin?'

Cassandra was waiting by the sitting room door, watching him in obvious concern. Just how long had he been standing there, locked in his thoughts, unaware of anything else?

With an effort he dragged his attention back to the present.

'Sorry. It's just rather weird knowing that I've lived here for the past month and I can't remember anything of it.'

'It must be,' she said, giving nothing away. 'Why don't you come and have this coffee? Ramón can't stay long...'

The sooner his brother left the better, as far as he was concerned. With Ramón there, acting like a guard dog, watching every word of the conversation, there was going to be no chance of Cassandra letting anything slip. He couldn't wait to be left alone with her and try to probe for answers. The time between now and then was going to seem far, far too long.

The time Joaquin's brother had spent with them had passed far too quickly, Cassie told herself as she stood watching, waiting until Ramón's car had totally disappeared from view before slowly shutting the door and going back, reluctantly, into the house.

She had tried everything she could to make him stay longer. Offering him another drink, food—anything to delay the time when, inevitably, he would leave and she would have to face the fact that she was now on her own with Joaquin and she had no idea at all how to behave.

She didn't even know how to face him, was terrified of looking him in the eyes, wondering just what she would see. And even worse was the thought that he would look into *her* face and see...

And see *what*?

That there was so much that she was keeping from him?

Could he sense the secrets that came between them, like smoke hanging in the air? Would he not rest until he had winkled them out of her, picking away at her defences until she gave everything away?

Or would he just watch her and wait, knowing when she was not telling the truth, when she was dodging the issue, knowing that one day, inevitably, she wouldn't be able to keep it all back any longer, and she would have to let it out.

And would that be worse than the distinct possibility that he could just wake up one morning—any morning—even tomorrow—and find that his memory had come back? That the missing month was all there, clear in his mind, in perfect recall. And what would she see in his face then? What sort of accusations would he throw at her—and would he even wait for the answers?

How could she live with the tension, the uncertainty, the fear? How could she get through each day not knowing what was going to happen next?

And what about the nights?

That was something she just wasn't ready to face until she felt a lot braver, and had managed to drag together some sort of composure. So she deliberately avoided going back into the room where she knew Joaquin was waiting for her, heading instead for the kitchen, finding herself an endless string of unimportant and largely unnecessary tasks to keep her occupied. She washed up the coffee mugs by hand instead of simply putting them in the dishwasher, washed and sliced a salad to go with their evening meal, wiped every possible surface within reach, set about mopping the floor...

'Are you trying to avoid me?'

Joaquin's voice, mild enough but with an edge that might

have been curiosity, or perhaps something else, came to her from the open door, making her jump in nervous shock.

He was standing in the doorway, dark and, to her already nervous mind, disturbingly dangerous. The dark bruise that had spread across his forehead was already turning into different colours, deep burgundy at the centre, yellow at the edges like some malign sunset, adding to the impression of menace.

'Avoid? N—no. Why would I want to do that?'

'I don't know—you tell me.'

This time it was definitely challenging, making her heart thud in uneasy response.

'I had things to do if we're going to eat soon.'

'To tell you the truth, I'm not that hungry. Except for two things.'

'What two things?'

Did she have to ask? Weren't they there, in the darkness of his eyes, the set, controlled expression on his face?

'Facts...'

'Oh, now you know I can't tell you anything. The doctors were insistent about that. We have to wait—'

'For my memory to come back; I know,' Joaquin supplied, his tone sending chills down her spine.

Forcing herself not to react, she turned her attention to an imaginary spot on the already immaculate worktop surface, rubbing at it hard with a cloth.

'And the other?'

'Oh, come on, Cassandra,' Joaquin mocked, sending even more shivers along every nerve, but in a very different way from before. 'You know. I want you.'

The cleaning cloth froze mid-rub and Cassie stared down at it, but blindly, seeing nothing.

He was right; she had known this was coming. But not so soon. Not yet! Not when she was still totally unprepared to handle it.

'That isn't a very good idea, is it?'

She jumped almost sky-high as strong, tanned fingers closed over her own hand, stilling the nervous movement and holding her there.

'Why not?'

She flicked a nervous, uncertain sidelong glance in his direction and then away again, meeting the black, searching eyes only for a moment. Her heart was racing in a way that had nothing to do with the shock of his sudden grab at her hand, but everything to do with the stinging awareness of the size and strength of his body so close to hers.

She could feel the heat of his skin where her arm touched him, seemed to be surrounded by the clean, intimate scent of his body, and he was so close that his breath caressed her cheek as he spoke, its warmth stirring her hair, drying her mouth.

'You—you know why!'

'No.'

The cloth was plucked from her nerveless fingers, tossed in the vague direction of the sink, and then he took hold of her arms, spinning her round so that she had no option but to face him. But she couldn't look up so as to meet his gaze, instead staring fixedly at the point where the open neck of his white shirt lay open revealing the bronze skin and muscular strength of his throat, and just the beginning of his broad chest.

Even that was bad enough.

Her fingers itched to touch, to slide in at the open edges of the shirt and feel the warm satin of his skin, the crisp curl of body hair under their tips. Her lips actually tingled, knowing that all she had to do was to purse them slightly, lean forward a little, and they would rest against the muscles, the sinews, under the tanned covering of his flesh. In spite of herself, she inhaled deeply, taking in the scent of him, drawing in as much of him as she could without actually making contact.

'Tell me why. And don't mention the damn doctors!'

That brought her head up, sharply, protest flashing in her eyes. She would have pulled away but the strength of his arms, linked apparently loosely, at the base of her spine held her back. If she pulled against it, she knew that that seemingly gentle hold would tighten. She would be held a prisoner, fighting a futile battle against his superior strength. And that would give too much away. Much more than she dared risk anyway.

'That just isn't fair and you know it. I *have* to mention the doctors—I don't have any alternative! They only let you home on the condition that I looked after you and in order to do that I have to follow their instructions—to the letter.'

Joaquin's silence made her even more uncomfortable than ever. He had narrowed his eyes until only the jet gleam showed through the curtain of long black lashes and his mouth had completely stopped smiling and was clamped into a thin, hard line. Every instinct she possessed warned of danger but she couldn't heed the caution. This was no longer a question of concern for herself, but for his health.

For that she was prepared to fight him as hard as she could.

'You were told to take things easy and I intend to make sure that you do just that! And I don't think that—that what you have in mind is taking it easy.'

She could almost read his train of thought in his face as a gleam started up in those newly opened eyes and a wicked grin played over the sensual mouth.

'It could be, if we let it.'

One strong hand strayed upwards, drifted over her hair, smoothly it softly, the tenderness of the gesture pulling at her heart.

'I could take it *very* easy...'

His proud head lowered very slowly, making her heart skip a beat as she guessed at his intentions. The soft, lingering pressure of his lips against the side of her temple, her ear, her cheek made her melt, swaying in towards him in spite of her resolution not to.

And that moment of weakness left her in no doubt at all that for all his calm demeanour, his subtle, sensual approach, Joaquin was hotly, heavily aroused, the bulge of his masculinity pressing tight against the black denim of his jeans.

'Joaquin…'

She struggled to find a voice with which to argue with him. She *had* to argue. She had no other choice.

'Cassandra, *querida*—I don't have to make any effort at all. If we were to go to bed…'

Once more his tormenting mouth teased at her nerves, caressing the line of her jaw, before moving to tantalise her lips, his tongue sliding out to trace around them delicately.

'And I'm sure that the stern doctors would approve of my taking to my bed so early in the evening…'

'No…' Cassie tried again, but her voice had no strength, no authority.

'Then you could do all the…'

That wicked mouth quirked up into the most sinful grin that he directed straight into her troubled blue eyes.

'All the work… And I could just lie back and think of Spain.'

The image that sprang into Cassie's mind at just the thought was so burningly erotic, making the heat rush through her veins, her head swim, so that she closed her eyes against the force of it. But that was a definite mistake. The sensual images persisted, projecting onto the back of her eyelids the impression of Joaquin lying back in the bed, and herself straddling him, both of them naked, her paler skin looking almost white in contrast to his long, bronzed body.

'Joaquin!' His name was a groan of effort, pushed from her by the struggle not to give in. 'Joaquin, *stop it*!'

'You stop me,' he challenged, the rich, dark sensuality

of his voice implying that he knew only too well that she would not.

She could feel his smile against her skin, just before those tantalising lips caressed again, moving away from her mouth and down...down, driving her to arch her neck in sensual response. The vee-necked dress she wore gave him access to the vulnerable spots at her throat and shoulders, something he immediately took advantage of.

His hands knew just where to go as well. Starting on the swell of her buttocks, they stroked and smoothed their way upwards, pressing her close to the straining heat of his erection as they went. At her breasts the knowing fingers cupped the soft weight, closing around them as the heat of his palms reached through to her delicate skin. And they traced tantalisingly erotic patterns over her curves, drawing provocative circles round and round her tightening nipples, tormenting her with the 'so near and yet so far' effect that came from feeling his touch through the fine cotton of her dress, the barely there lace of her bra.

'Joaquin...'

This time his name was a sigh. A sound in which she could hear her own control evaporating, her resistance ebbing away.

Clearly Joaquin could hear it too. She felt his tiny laugh of triumph in response against her shoulder blade and shivered in instinctive reaction as it was followed by the faint graze of his teeth over the sensitive surface of her skin.

'So stop me,' he muttered thickly, the rough, fraying edge to the words revealing how fast his hold over his own passion was slipping. 'If you really mean it, say the word. But say it now, damn you, before it's too late.'

Say the word.

The hoarse-voiced command barely penetrated the hungry haze inside Cassie's head. Passion had scrambled her brain, leaving it impossible to think clearly.

The word.

What word?

What should she say if she wanted him to stop?

And she did want him to stop.

Or did she?

She knew she should tell him to stop. There was too much danger, too many complications if she went down this sensually enticing path. Too much to lose.

But she still couldn't find the word.

The restless clamour of her senses had drowned out the functioning of her brain. Somehow the importance of common sense and self-preservation didn't weigh enough to outbalance the hungry need for this man. Perhaps if she hadn't been apart from him for that week, if she hadn't missed his lovemaking already...

'I knew it.'

The triumph in his voice was even richer and darker now, and hearing it sent a tiny chill shivering through Cassie, tempering her ardour for just a moment. Reluctantly she opened her eyes, focused on the dark, stunning face above hers.

And was shaken back into reality by the sight of the discoloured, spreading bruise on his forehead, reminding her sharply of his injury.

'No!'

She had no hesitation in finding the word now. It jumped from her lips a second before she stiffened in his arms, drawing herself back, struggling to get away.

'No, Joaquin. You can't—we mustn't!'

'Mustn't!'

Black rage flared in his eyes, turning them into deep, blazing fires that scorched with every searing glance he turned on her.

'Can't? Why *not*?'

But the brief moment of shock had been enough to loosen his hold on her, giving her just enough liberty to twist free and take herself away, across the kitchen and out of reach. Reacting rather than thinking, she moved to put the kitchen table between herself and him. Not so much for her protection from Joaquin, though the fury in his eyes was dangerous enough, but more as a defence against herself and her own weak impulses.

If he tempted her just once more, she knew she would give in. She was only human, and so desperately vulnerable where he was concerned. With the table between them, the time it took to walk round it might just give her space to have much-needed second thoughts.

'Cassie?'

What the hell was wrong with her? Joaquin asked himself. What had happened to make her change her mind, behave this way?

She didn't usually do anything like this. Cassandra wasn't a tease; never had been. At least, the Cassandra he had known had never been a tease.

Just what the devil had happened in that missing month? Was there something he really should know? Something important?

Okay, so the bang on the head had scrambled his brain, but he remembered the Cassandra he had been living with before he'd lost those weeks. Or thought he did. And she had never been one to pull back, to say no. That had always been the best thing about their relationship.

So could it have changed so much in a month?

'Just what in the devil's name is wrong? Why can't we go to bed? We live together.'

'We mustn't...'

She *wasn't* teasing. Her white face and dark, shadowed eyes told him that, far from playing with him, she was deadly serious. Something had shaken her badly.

And because of his stupid head, he didn't know what.

'Why the hell not?'

He took a step forward, then stopped when immediately she stiffened, edging back herself, away from him. Oh, she tried to conceal the fact, but he'd caught the small, uncontrollable movement and it shook him rigid. He'd never seen Cassandra back away from him before—at least, he *thought* he hadn't.

'Why not?' he asked again, more quietly but no less intently.

'Because—because I told the doctors I'd look after you. Because I promised.'

'And is that all?'

Could that really be all it was? Had she really got into such a state over that?

'Of course that's all! What else could there be? You're only just out of hospital and I gave the doctors my word I wouldn't let you overdo things and...and...'

'All right, I understand,' Joaquin cut in sharply when she began to stumble over her words, clearly upset. 'I never meant— Oh, hell, Cassandra, I'm sorry! I never thought...'

'Too damn right you didn't think,' she came back at him, but he was relieved to see that she had relaxed a little, the tension leaving her shoulders, her back and neck held less rigidly erect. 'You never do—except with one part of you.'

Her glance down towards his groin was both a delight and a torment. Delight because it revealed that he hadn't been mistaken in the Cassandra he recalled. That she was still the gloriously uninhibited, sensual woman who had shared his bed and brought him so much pleasure over the time they had been together.

But at the same time there was a bitter torment in knowing that, in spite of his efforts to subdue it, his wilful body was instantly responding to even her glance. That even under the slightest of provocations, he was hot and hard and hungry in an instant, the ache of unappeased desire threatening to become an agony before too long.

And that physical discomfort gave him a sudden, blindingly clear insight into the way Cassandra was feeling now. She too must have experienced the frustration of breaking off lovemaking when her senses were already fully aroused. And she *had* been aroused. He had known it. Sensed it in the yielding suppleness of her body, the way she had swayed towards him, the way her mouth had opened under his and she had returned his kiss with every ounce of the intensity that he had put into it for her.

She had wanted him as much as he'd wanted her. And breaking off as abruptly as she had done must have left every nerve in her body screaming, her senses desperate for appeasement.

And she had had to break away because of concern for his health. No wonder she had reacted so violently.

'I'm sorry,' he said again. 'I understand.'

Right now he really *did* understand. Along with the ache of frustration, an uncomfortable pounding had started up inside his head. If he needed any indication of the fact that Cassandra was right and he had been pushing things, then that was it.

'Okay,' he said abruptly. 'We'll eat instead.'

The look she turned on him was pure Cassandra, exasperation evident in the flash of her eyes, the irritated exclamation. But at least this time he knew what was going on, and recognised what was pushing her. And knew that she recognised what had brought about his hasty capitulation.

'You see!' she exclaimed. 'I was right!'

'Yeah,' Joaquin admitted wryly. 'You were right. I think I'll go and sit quietly by the pool for a while.'

'You do that.'

It was so prim and smug that it tugged at the corners of his mouth, quirking them into a reluctant grin.

'And don't gloat,' he flung at her.

Cassandra's smile was instant, wide and spontaneous.

'Would I?' she teased. 'You've admitted I was right— what more do I need? Now go and sit down.'

'*Sì, senorita!*'

His response was light, flippant, relieved. This was the Cassandra he remembered. The Cassandra he wanted in his life. That other woman was a stranger; one he didn't understand.

But perhaps *he* was the one who was behaving like a stranger. Perhaps he had been so shaken up by the accident—and he had to admit that being in hospital for the first time in his life had rocked him badly—that he wasn't thinking straight.

Cassandra wasn't the one who had changed but him.

'I promise. For the rest of the night, I will do exactly as you say. Follow the doctors' orders to the letter.'

'If I could believe that, I'd relax a lot more.'

It was said with such feeling that he couldn't stop himself. He had to reassure her. Had to let her know that he understood, and appreciated, her behaviour.

Walking over to her, he reached out a hand, put it under her chin, and lifted her face to his so that wide, brilliant blue eyes locked sharply with deep, intent black.

'Believe it,' he declared huskily. 'To the letter.'

And then, because he just had, he dropped a firm, swift kiss onto her mouth, just enough pressure to communicate how much he meant what he'd said. And knew immediately that it was a mistake.

His still-hungry body wasn't lying quiet as he had thought. The carnal craving that he had for this woman had only been subdued, not suppressed. And as soon as his mouth touched hers it sprang to hard and brutal life again, clawing at him mercilessly, making him want to grab at her, fling her to the floor, tear that dress…

No!

He had to get out of here. Get away and calm down, cool down. Think of something—*anything* else.

He had promised her he would do as she asked. And he'd meant it. So now he had to stick to it.

Ruthlessly suppressing the hungry clamour inside him,

he looked her deep in the eyes one last time before dropping a kiss down on the delightful, faintly upturned tip of her nose. Just a brief butterfly kiss. There and then away again, because he didn't trust himself not to do anything else if he lingered.

'To the letter,' he promised again. Then made himself walk away, heading for the door out into the garden.

It was as he stepped out in to the shadowy warmth of the evening that he turned to glance back and saw her still standing where he had left her, watching him, wide-eyed. Her right hand had been lifted to her mouth and was covering her lips, fingertips pressed against their softness.

But it was something in her expression that caught on his nerves, jagged and twisted uncomfortably.

And suddenly all the hard-won peace of mind that he had fought for vanished, evaporating swiftly, and he knew once again that nagging feeling of edginess and uncertainty that had so unsettled him all day.

Cassie didn't know how she managed to prepare the meal without slicing into her finger or putting salt into the fruit salad. She couldn't force her mind to concentrate, and the knowledge that this was only the beginning was what made things so much worse.

She had managed to deal with things this time, had got Joaquin to understand this once—but what would happen next time?

And there would be a next time, of that she was sure. Joaquin might have seemed understanding and reasonable tonight, but she couldn't rely on him being in the same mood again. For one thing, it was the lingering after-effects of his accident that had pushed him into an unexpectedly swift capitulation. But with each day that passed he would grow stronger, getting his health back as quickly and efficiently as he did anything.

The bruise on his head wasn't likely to be a problem for very much longer.

The memory loss was a very different matter indeed. And it kept her trapped in that very uncomfortable cleft stick for as long as it took for the events of the past four weeks to come back into Joaquin's mind.

Just how uncomfortable her situation could become was brought home sharply to her at the end of the evening. And it hit her all the harder because of the way she had actually managed to relax in the end.

Joaquin had stuck strictly to his promise. He would follow her orders to the letter, he'd said—and that was just what he did.

As soon as she said that the meal was ready, he came to help her carry plates through into the dining room. Then he joined her at the table, ate what she put in front of him, stuck strictly to mineral water for himself, but offered to open a bottle of wine for her. An offer that Cassie decided it was more than wise to refuse. She needed all her wits about her at the moment, and, although the thought of the relaxing effects of a little alcohol were appealing, there was always the danger that, feeling as uptight as she did, she might indulge in one glass too many, relax way too much— and let slip things that she really should keep to herself.

But in the end she found that she didn't really need the wine. Joaquin kept the conversation light, and on strictly neutral topics, never once straying into controversial or problematic territory. He managed to steer his way perfectly between the twin problems of assuming too much and behaving like the lover he had been, and that of being almost a complete stranger, so that the evening had to be spent dancing round each other mentally, not knowing how much to say, how much to reveal.

It was only later, when she had gone to bed and was lying wakeful in the darkness, that Cassie realised that the behaviour that had made her feel so much better during the evening should in fact have acted as a warning. It revealed that Joaquin was very much alert to the way she was feeling. That he had noticed her unease, and was determined, for that night at least, to ease it. As a result he had lulled her into what might well be a totally false sense of security.

But by the time that darkness had fallen and the silence of the night had gathered round them, she had just been so thankful that they had got through the evening without any more unpleasantness or a problem that she would have had trouble explaining, that such worrying thoughts hadn't entered her head.

In fact, she'd been so relieved to find that the time had passed so pleasantly that she'd never even thought twice about saying, as she'd watched Joaquin's eyelids grow heavy, drooping over the jet brilliance of his eyes, and his long body slump lower in his chair: 'You're getting tired. I think it's time that you were in bed.'

She knew how worn out he must really be when he didn't even rise to the provocation, but simply nodded slowly and murmured, 'That would be a good idea.'

'Well, then, why don't you go on up? I'll tidy things away here and follow.'

Again, no protest. Could it really be that easy? After the way he had behaved earlier, she very much doubted it, but she wasn't going to question too strongly—not tonight. She was worn out too, though probably not as exhausted as Joaquin must be on his first day out of hospital. The strain of the past seventy-two hours was catching up with her, and she had spent long hours in the hospital, sitting in a chair by Joaquin's bed, and then had barely slept when she'd got back to Ramón's flat.

Stretching wearily and yawning so widely that she felt her jaw would crack, she switched off the lights and made her way to the stairs, plodding slowly up them, thinking longingly of sinking into her bed. Joaquin would probably be asleep already. He had looked so exhausted that he must have crashed out as soon as his head hit the pillow.

He hadn't.

She reached the top of the stair and turned to go along the landing, then jumped in fright as she became aware of the tall, dark, silent figure leaning against the wall in the shadows, waiting for her.

'Joaquin! Oh, you gave me such a fright! What is it? Why are you—is something wrong?'

'I don't know,' was the response, in a voice that turned her blood to ice in her veins and made her throat close up so tight that it was difficult to breathe. 'You tell me.'

Straightening up and taking a step forward, he kicked open the nearest door. The door to a bedroom—her bedroom, she noted with a sickening lurch of her stomach. The bedroom she had chosen to sleep in tonight, knowing she could not possibly share a bed with Joaquin under the circumstances.

As the door swung open it revealed what Joaquin must have seen, the details that betrayed her, the silent evidence that revealed her plans. Her nightdress and robe lay on the bed, her wash bag on the dresser. She could only be intensely grateful that she had pushed the case she'd brought back from Ramón's firmly to the back of the wardrobe so that he didn't realise she had only just managed to unpack part of her luggage before he and his brother had appeared downstairs. And that all of it was in this room—not the one she had once shared with him.

'I...' she began but her voice failed her hopelessly.

'You?' Joaquin questioned cynically, his carved face just a cold mask of contempt and barely controlled cold fury. 'So just what explanation were you planning on giving me for this? I take it you do have one?'

'Of course I do.'

The realisation that there was nothing more revealing than her nightdress on show gave a new strength to her words, giving her the courage to face him with a touch of defiance.

'And you'd know what it is if you were thinking straight!'

Joaquin scowled darkly, glaring at her ferociously.

'Don't tell me—the doctors' orders again?'

'Got it in one!' Cassie retorted sharply. 'And you'll also have to admit that it makes sense.'

The cynically sceptical look he turned on her declared that he found that very unlikely, but she swallowed hard and forced herself to continue.

'You're just out of hospital. You need a good night's sleep and for that you need to be undisturbed.'

'And you'll disturb me?'

'I—I might. Or you might let yourself be disturbed by me. Oh, come on, Joaquin!' she risked a protest. 'You promised me that you'd do as I said.'

'I know I did—and I have. But this—'

He broke off abruptly, glowering at her darkly. Cassie held her breath in apprehension, not knowing what on earth she would do if he flat out refused to co-operate.

But Joaquin must have been even more tired and out of sorts than she had anticipated, because just as she had drawn in a breath to argue further, to try and persuade him to understand, he gave a deep sigh and lifted his shoulders in a shrug of concession.

'All right. If that's what you were told, I suppose I can't argue.'

'It was!' Cassie assured him, crossing her fingers against the small white lie. 'Doctors' orders.'

'And I promised…'

'Yes, you did.'

Still he held out, looking into the   black eyes going from the bed to her taut, anxious face and back again.

'All right, then,' he said at last. 'I'll go along with this for now—because I promised. But let me make one thing plain...'

When he hesitated Cassie froze, knowing she wasn't going to like what was coming.

'I'll go along with this for tonight. And only tonight. Tomorrow is another day and tomorrow I want things back to normal—or I'll want to know why.'

CHAPTER NINE

JOAQUIN arrived back at the house in a mood that had him ready to do battle. He had had enough of messing about, not asking questions, avoiding the issues, and tonight he was going to get some answers.

It was either that or explode.

He had spent the day out at one of the vineyards, dealing with business, talking vines, blends, wine, in an effort to distract his mind from the suspicions and fears that were a constant nag inside his head, worrying and fretting at him until his thoughts were one great ache of unease. One that nothing he did seemed to improve.

He'd taken the wrong approach on the first night home, he admitted that now, if only to himself. Challenging Cassandra like that, and threatening her with confrontation, had been quite the wrong way to go. He'd known it as soon as he'd seen her head come up, the flash in her eyes, that defiant chin tilted in rebellion. And the long night in which, in spite of his exhaustion, he hadn't been able to sleep had only confirmed his feeling even more.

Whatever had happened between himself and Cassandra during the time his mind had lost, playing the autocrat and dictating the rules was not likely to help. Continue to push her down that route, and he was heading for disaster.

So he had moved onto another tack, deciding to see just how far she would take this. And for how long.

'I realise I was being pigheaded about things,' he told her the next morning. You're only acting on those doctors' orders. And trying to do what you believe is best for me. I should appreciate your concern—I do...'

It would have sounded better if he could have projected

an ounce more sincerity into his voice, but that was more than he could manage. Oh, he appreciated her concern all right, but it infuriated the hell out of him at the same time. To his mind, sleeping apart was taking things just too far.

And that showed in his tone, which was cool and stiff in a way that he knew would rile her, setting her teeth on edge and provoking her own temper.

He was right. He saw the way her jaw tightened, as if to hold back the angry retort that she almost let out. And her own tone matched his, ice for ice, when she responded.

'Nice of you to say so. Believe it or not, I do have your best interests at heart.'

'I know—and I do believe it, so that's why I'm not going to put any pressure on you. If you seriously think that sleeping in separate rooms is absolutely necessary, I'll go along with it—for now. For your sake.'

That brought those blue eyes to his face in a rush of surprise, the frown that drew her pale eyebrows together revealing her consternation.

'For *my* sake?' she echoed disbelievingly.

'I wouldn't want you to feel uneasy about things—or to push you into something that you truly felt was a bad move in your concern for my health after the accident...'

He emphasised those last words subtly, wanting her to know that he wasn't truly convinced by this 'for his health' argument. If she had something to say, then he just wished to hell that she'd come right out and say it, instead of playing this pussyfooting game that left him floundering in the dark.

'So I'll leave it up to you. I've never forced a woman into my bed, and I don't intend to start now. You'll come when you're ready. When it feels right to you. I want you with me—you *know* I want you, but I want you willing. So I'll wait.'

'Thank you.'

It was very quiet, flat and unemotional. She might have

been talking about the price of the fish they were having for dinner, for all the intonation she put into it.

And that piqued him savagely, rattling all his instincts for danger again, and reviving his darkest suspicions.

'I know you'll be worth waiting for. That's one thing that no blow to the head could ever make me forget. What we have is something special. Something few people find together, and I don't want to spoil it by rushing at it like a bull at a gate.'

'Of course not.'

This time there was a definite undercurrent of something that brought his teeth together in a snap to bite back the angry response that rose to his lips. He had determined on being calm and controlled and right now he was beginning to feel neither. That comment about the 'something special' they shared, and the heated images it threw up in his mind, had woken his barely controlled libido. And with the blood rushing fast to a more basic part of his anatomy, thinking clearly and keeping a grip on his temper weren't the easiest things in the world.

He had to get out of here before he lost his grip completely.

'So we'll leave it like that,' he managed, knowing it was even more cold and clipped than before as a result of the struggle with his innermost feelings. 'I'll wait—for now. But I'm not a patient man, *querida*. I won't wait for ever. You're my lover, and I want you back in my bed, where you belong.'

He'd walked away then, Joaquin remembered. Walked away while he still could, and still keep his grip on his temper, his tongue, and his hunger for her. And the only thing that had helped him turn around and walk had been the total conviction that really saying he would wait had been an unnecessary political manoeuvre. He could probably have got by without ever having said anything of the sort.

Cassie wouldn't wait long before she was back in his arms, back in his bed. She wasn't that sort of woman. She was an ardent, passionate, sensual creature. One who was as hot for him as he was for her. And that being so, she would come to him just as soon as she possibly could.

She might wait one more night, purely for show, to make her point. But not much longer. And definitely no more than two.

He'd been quite sure about that, smug even, so it had hit him like a blow between the eyes to find that his confident prediction had not been fulfilled.

The answer to the question of just how long Cassandra could keep this up was, it appeared, infinitely.

Oh, she always had a reason. He looked tired. It had been a long day. She had a headache—a *headache*! Or there was some work she had to do—and of course she couldn't do that work during the day, because she was looking after him. And no amount of persuasion would convince her that he damn well didn't need looking after. Not any more.

Today it was a week since he had come out of hospital. A week in which he had had no ill effects from the accident—apart, of course, from those infuriatingly missing memories. He felt well—he felt fine. The lingering headache had faded along with most of the bruising, and he was once more fighting fit.

And frustrated as hell.

But only this morning, when he was dressing to go to work for the first time since the accident, his hand had caught on the pocket of one of his jackets. The unexpected little bulge had intrigued him, making him pause and, frowning in curiosity, push his hand into the pocket, to investigate just what had caused it.

What he had pulled out had rocked him so much that he felt as if he had been physically picked up and shaken until he was dizzy. It made him reconsider everything he had been working on, told him something totally unexpected about the four weeks he had had erased from his memory.

And it made him decide that he couldn't afford to wait any longer. That tonight, if Cassandra showed no inclination to move back into his room—*their* room—where she belonged—he was going to find out why.

To hell with the consequences.

'Cassandra!'

He called her name as soon as he got through the door.

'Cassandra, where are you?'

No answer.

The next moment he almost reeled against the wall as a weird, buzzing sensation, almost like pins and needles inside his mind, shot through his brain.

He'd had this once before, he recalled. That swimming, swirling feeling that he'd had on the first day when he'd come back from the hospital. It came with the impression that his subconscious was reaching for something, grabbing at some faint echo of memory. Something he should recall but couldn't.

Shaking his head, he called again.

'Cassie!'

'In here!'

She'd called from the lounge. For some reason he'd thought—almost anticipated—that she would be upstairs. He'd even turned towards the staircase, only to be stopped, turned back, by the sound of her voice.

'I thought we might eat—'

He ceased speaking abruptly, silenced by her raised hand. She was on the telephone, speaking to someone at the other end of the line.

'Yes, he's here now,' she said, sounding rather uncomfortable.

It immediately set Joaquin's nerves jangling. He'd already spent a week wondering if something was wrong, wondering *what* was wrong, wondering if he was imagining things, and cursing the damned doctors' orders that meant he couldn't just come out and ask. As a result he was getting jumpy over the tiniest little thing.

'Who is it?' he demanded.

'Ramón. He—he wants to come over.'

'No!'

His vehemence surprised even himself. He didn't want his brother here. Certainly not tonight. Tonight was his and Cassandra's—alone. He didn't want anything to interfere with that.

'I'd like him to come...'

'No way!'

'But, Joaquin, he's concerned about you.'

Demonios, but was he condemned to reading extra meanings into everything she said? Had she meant to imply that Ramón had good reasons for being concerned—ones that Cassandra too knew all about?

He really was getting paranoid!

'Tell him he's no reason to worry about me. I'm fine.'

'But he'd—'

'I said no!'

For a moment he thought she was going to fight him on this. The rebellious set to her sexy mouth, the carefully blanked-out glare, seemed to warn of open mutiny. But then she sighed and twisted her mouth slightly.

'Did you hear that, Ramón?' she said dryly, addressing the telephone once more. 'He says no! Your brother is not at home to visitors... What? Yes, I know! And you know I know.'

The last was said in a wryly confiding aside that raised all the little hairs on the back of Joaquin's neck. Losing control of his already precarious temper, he strode forward, snatching the receiver from Cassandra's hand with a rough, jerky movement.

'Cassandra and I don't want visitors. Not tonight. Not for any night for a long time to come.'

He slammed the phone back down onto its rest, earning himself a furious glare from those bright blue eyes.

'And just what was all that about?' she demanded sharply.

'I don't want visitors.'

'That much is obvious. But who the devil gave you the right to speak for me? "Cassandra and I don't want visitors",' she quoted sarcastically. '"Cassandra and I—don't you think you might have done me the courtesy of *asking*?"'

'It's my house!'

'It's *our* house!' she flung back. 'At least, I thought it was! And I would have liked to see Ramón.'

'Well, I don't want him here. I have plans for tonight.'

Or was that why she wanted his brother here? Because she knew—or suspected—what his plans might be and she wanted some form of distraction from them?

Did she want Ramón here as some sort of shield against what she believed might happen? Or did she want him here because she *wanted to see Ramón*? And which was worse?

He supposed that those came under the heading of 'questions that must not be asked', but there were others that he could ask—and would. Particularly, if the time and the mood were right, one very important one.

'And I can just guess what those "plans for tonight" include.'

It looked as if her time of indulgence was over, Cassie admitted to herself. The temporary truce that Joaquin had surprised her by declaring was over. He wasn't exactly making ultimatums—at least, not yet. But what patience he had had was obviously running out fast. He was going to want some answers to some very awkward questions. And she had no idea at all what she was going to find to say to him. She hadn't been feeling particularly well for the last couple of days and an argument was the last thing she wanted.

'And just what is wrong with that? We're lovers. We live together—just what is wrong in my wanting to make love to my woman?'

Because it wouldn't be *making love*, Cassie wanted to reply, but she hastily bit back the dangerous words. To use them meant that she was moving into forbidden territory, the sort of area that was littered with land-mines, some of them totally hidden from view, but liable to explode right in her face if she so much as strayed near to them.

'I—' she tried but he jumped in on her with the speed of a leaping tiger.

'And don't try that "doctors' orders" garbage again. You know I saw the specialist yesterday and he said that, apart from the memory loss, there was nothing to get concerned about at all.'

Nothing except what that memory loss was concealing, Cassie thought miserably. She no longer knew whether each night, alone in her room, she prayed that when the morning came Joaquin would have regained all the memories he had lost so that she was no longer trapped in this impossible world of half-truths. Or did she hope that when she woke he would still *not* have remembered—so that she could continue at least with the sort of peace they had between them, even if that was based on half-lies?

She tried as hard as she dared to get him to remember. She'd talked about Ramón, even invited Joaquin's brother over a couple of times to try and jog his memory. She'd pointedly left the calendar open at June, even though the month had now come to an end, in the hope that the date might remind him. But it seemed that nothing short of telling him outright would do that. And the doctor's advice was strongly against that.

'I know,' she said carefully. 'And I'm glad that you're well.'

'So why don't we go out tonight to celebrate? I booked a table at Zelesta's.'

Her favourite restaurant. The one at which she had been supposed to join him for the vitally important business meeting on that fateful Friday evening.

'I—I don't think that would be a good idea.'

'And why not?'

Because she knew what was coming, that was why not.

But then of course she'd been expecting it. She'd been on tenterhooks all week, her stomach clenching on a twist of nerves each time Joaquin had said that he was calling it a night, or she had known she couldn't suppress a yawn, or stay awake a moment longer. She'd always known that her luck couldn't last. That at some point his patience must run out. But why now? Why tonight? What on earth had put him in this mood?

And what was it going to lead to?

Would they sit opposite each other in a restaurant, lighted candles on the table, polished silver and crystal glassware gleaming in the soft light—and talk about...?

About what?

About living together and the wonderful days, the glorious nights they shared? About how happy they were? How everything was perfect? Or at least how Joaquin believed that everything was perfect.

Would they talk about their future and the plans, the dreams they had—together?

Memories of that last morning, the morning before she had left him, swirled into her mind in a torrent of hateful images. She heard again his voice saying, 'I told you I don't do commitment'; saw the blank lack of emotion in his eyes; felt the tearing pain of knowing that she could never be to him what he was to her. And knew that she could never go through with the sort of evening of courtship and sophisticated seduction that he so obviously had planned.

'I just don't think...'

She wouldn't be able to eat a thing. It would choke her. Tension would close her throat, making it impossible to swallow, and she would have to sit there, locked in misery, unable to speak, feeling as if the doctors had clamped a muzzle over her mouth with their ruling that she must keep silent on the events of the four weeks that were missing from Joaquin's memory.

Then, when the evening was over, she knew that Joaquin would no longer be prepared to wait. That he would expect her to go to bed with him, or want to know the reason why.

And it was that *reason why* that she couldn't give to him.

'I mean—'

Inspiration struck and she grabbed at it in desperation, thankful for any way of escape.

'I think that it would be a pity to waste the meal I have planned. I've prepared most of it already…'

The slanting, sceptically suspicious glance that he turned on her had her improvising fast, embroidering on the few basic, factual details.

'I thought you'd like a paella?'

That was an important plus point. Paella was Joaquin's favourite dish and one she hadn't cooked for him in a while.

'I always like paella,' he drawled, his tone giving away as little as his expressionless, watchful face.

'And I thought we could eat out by the pool—it's going to be a lovely evening.'

'You've done a lot of thinking.'

To judge by the faint glimmer of a smile, he clearly believed that she was planning this romantic evening *à deux* for much the same reasons as he had booked the restaurant. His next words confirmed as much.

'And our thoughts seem to be running on the same lines. Okay.'

He stretched lazily, pushing both hands through his glossy ebony hair.

'Do you want some help in the kitchen?'

'No—no need…'

If he came into the kitchen he would realise just how far from the truth her statement that she had already prepared most of the meal had been.

'I can manage. Why don't you take a shower?'

'I'll do that. It's been a pretty sultry day, and I could do with freshening up. I won't be long.'

He was turning towards the door when he stopped suddenly, swung back, and fixed her with a wide, wicked smile, a devilish gleam lighting up in the midnight darkness of his eyes.

'Unless of course you'd like to join me?'

That smile, the glitter in his eyes, were pure temptation, and in spite of herself Cassie felt all that was female in her respond to them in an instant. Her heartbeat kicked up, heating her blood and making it throb along her nerves. Her mouth dried, yearning to press itself against the sensual curve of his. It would be so easy to say yes... In fact she had opened her mouth to do just that before a savage reproof from her sense of self-preservation brought her up short, pushing other words into her thoughts.

'If I did that then the meal would never be ready.'

That roguish grin grew wider, even more dazzling, brilliant white teeth gleaming sharply against the dark tan of his skin.

'To tell you the truth, I wouldn't mind. I have other appetites that are just as pressing—more so.'

He was reaching for her as he spoke. Another second and he would have caught hold of her wrist, dragging her into the confines of his arms, holding her tight against him.

'I don't think so.'

Somehow she managed to make it sound flippant, even flirtatious. And some sixth sense made her move at just the right moment, dodging his grasping hand, putting an extra distance between them.

'I know you when you're hungry—and it isn't a pretty sight! So you go and take that shower and I'll prepare a meal that will save me from having my head bitten off later.'

His unsmiling stillness made her hold her breath. Would he let it go at that or press her further?

A moment later, her tautly held shoulders slumped again in relief as Joaquin nodded acquiescence.

'Okay,' he said, calmly enough, but there was something in his eyes that promised he would not be so easily distracted later, that he would think up a punishment that was suitable to fit the crime he believed she had committed. 'We'll play it your way—for now.'

She'd won this round, Cassie told herself as she watched him stride up the stairs and out of sight. Or at least earned herself a reprieve. So why didn't she feel as if that were the case? Why was her mood as low as if she'd suffered the worst defeat possible? She was handling this the only way she knew how!

Why was she doing it? It would be so easy to follow him upstairs. To undress, to go into the bathroom, open the glass door to the shower cubicle and slip inside to join him...

And she *wanted* to do it. That was the cruellest irony of all. She *wanted* to be with him, wanted to sleep with him, wanted him to make love to her.

Which was the real sting in the tail. She wanted him to make *love* to her. And he wouldn't. All he wanted was to sleep with her, and she couldn't sleep with him and have it mean nothing. And surely when Joaquin regained his memory—and recalled his suspicions of Ramón—when he looked back at the way that she had turned down his insulting offer of marriage, the way he had stormed out of Ramón's apartment, then he would be furious with her. He would feel used. He would think that she had come to his bed because—because...

Cassie choked back a sob.

Because since his accident she could no longer go to Ramón's.

What was it he had said that night at his brother's apartment?

'Are you so insatiable that you've gone from my bed to my brother's in less than a week?'

Only now he would think that she had done it in reverse, going from Ramón's bed to his.

No. She couldn't let that happen again. Couldn't bear it to happen. She was far better off following her original plan and focusing her attention firmly on making the meal. She hadn't been kidding when she'd talked of the moods Joaquin got into when he was hungry.

She might have snatched the idea of the special meal out of the air in desperation and the hope of avoiding the horror of the restaurant that Joaquin had planned on, but perhaps she could turn it round to her advantage after all. She would cook the paella and they would share it—and then later they could talk...

She would try to jolt his memory once again. Try to make him think of the night before she had left him. To see if she could get him to remember.

She would have to tell him the whole truth. About the problems that had come between them, at least. It was the only way. And it wouldn't actually go against the doctors' orders. It wasn't something that had happened only in the time he had lost. It had been growing in her heart before that.

She would tell him of the way she had been feeling, what had driven her to feel she had no alternative but to leave him. She'd tell him of all the doubts and fears that had been swirling in her mind, the way she had felt he was about to end their relationship and how she had felt forced into considering her own pre-emptive strike.

Then at least if—when—he remembered, he would know *why* she had behaved as she had. He would know why she

had gone, leaving behind that note, why she had moved in
with Ramón. And although he might not want her back, at
least he would not hate his brother as he had when he had
stormed out of Ramón's apartment. She would not have
that on her conscience.

But for now she would cook. And she forced herself to
head into the kitchen, pulling out pans, bowls, ingredients
with an excessive clatter simply to try and drown out the
drumming sound of the shower upstairs.

She wasn't going to *think*.

But she couldn't stop herself. She couldn't help imagining Joaquin's hard, bronzed body standing under the
warm spray of the shower, the water cascading over his
lean frame, down the long, straight line of his back, over
the tight, male buttocks, around…

'Ow!'

It was a sharp exclamation of pain and automatically she
put her finger into her mouth, sucking to ease the pain
where the juice of the pepper she had been slicing had got
into the nick she had made in the skin.

Oh, who was she kidding? She didn't want to be here!
What she wanted was to be upstairs, with Joaquin, in
Joaquin's arms.

She wanted Joaquin, no matter what the aftermath might
be, no matter what the cost.

If having her in his bed was what Joaquin most wanted
right at this moment—it was what she wanted too. So why
was she denying both of them? If nothing else, she would
have tonight.

Tonight and any extra time that fate allowed her before
the missing weeks returned to Joaquin's brain and she was
forced to accept…accept what?

Well, she told herself, she would tackle that when it
came.

It was only when she found her hand reaching out for
the door—the door to Joaquin's bedroom—that she reali-

sed, with a devastating sense of shock, that even while she had been thinking, arguing with herself, justifying her thoughts, her body had been acting independently and she was already upstairs, and on the landing outside Joaquin's room. The room they had once shared in happier times.

The decision was made then, she told herself. And the truth was that she could no more make herself turn round and walk away, go back down the stairs, than she could fly to the moon.

This was what she wanted. What she needed. What her hungry body needed—and what her lonely heart most wanted in all the world.

She opened the door and went in, crossing the bedroom swiftly, not looking to right or left for fear of distraction or second thoughts. She shed her clothes as she went. Dropping them carelessly onto the rich blue carpet and leaving them where they fell, like a trail of pastel colour showing where she had been.

The shower was still running and the bathroom was full of steam. Steam also clouded the glass doors into the shower cabinet but through the misted walls she could see Joaquin. See his tall, lean frame, the intense black of his water-soaked hair, the deep bronze of his skin. The details of his body were blurred but she didn't need to see to picture the honed strength of the straight shoulders and long back, the muscles rippling as his arms lifted to clear the water from his face, the narrow waist and hips, the taut buttocks and powerful, hair-darkened legs. Her throat tightened, her mouth drying at just the thought.

He had his back to her, his face turned up to the shower head, and she knew that he wasn't even aware of her presence; the sound of the door opening drowned in the rush of the water.

'Now or never,' she told herself, the words propelling her forward. 'Now or never.'

Opening the door as little as she possibly could, she slipped inside.

Joaquin sensed her arrival immediately, the whisper of cooler air on his skin making him whirl around and stand, black eyes fixed on her face, just looking at her.

'Well, hi,' was all he said.

But that look made her feel beautiful and special, sexy and wanted, and somehow cherished. And it was all she could possibly have hoped for at this moment. She would never have dared to dream of anything more, let alone ask for it.

'Hi...' she managed, soft as a sigh.

Then he opened his arms and she went into them like a homing bird, and felt them close around her, warm and strong and, for now at least, very, very right.

CHAPTER TEN

HE HAD wanted her so much for so long, Joaquin thought
hazily through the rush of blood pounding in his head. So
much longer, it seemed, than the week he had spent sticking
strictly to her rules and avoiding all intimate contact. So
that when she finally came to him like this, warm and willing and oh, so welcome, he truly believed that there was
no way he was going to be able to hold back.

His hunger was so wild, so fierce that he felt he couldn't
restrain it in any way. It wouldn't be reined in, but wanted
to break out, wild and fierce and hungry as hell.

In his dreams, through the long, solitary nights when he
had slept alone in the bed they had once shared, he had
made love to Cassandra so ardently, so passionately, that
he'd woken with his heart still thudding, his blood carnally
hot and his senses screaming for appeasement of their hunger fast and *now*.

He had thought that whenever—if ever—Cassandra let
him touch her again, then his passion would surely spiral
out of control. That he would need only a touch of her
hand, the sweet scent of her skin, the soft pressure of her
mouth on his, to reach the point of no return. That he would
take her hard and fast, and that even as he tumbled back
to earth after the mind-blowing explosion of his climax he
would feel the insatiable hunger start to grow again, demanding more and more and more.

But from the moment that he had turned and seen her
standing there, just inside the door to the shower cubicle,
everything had changed. Every thought had flown from his
head, his mouth and throat had dried, and he had felt as

gauche and awkward as a young boy faced with his first ever experience of a woman.

Her blonde hair hung loose about her shoulders, her glorious body was totally naked and flushed pink from the heat of the shower.

Or was it from embarrassment?

Surely not. After their twelve months together, what reason could Cassandra have to feel embarrassed with him?

But, hell, if he could feel ill at ease and unsure, as he did, then why not? Because the truth was that he didn't know what to do. This sudden reversal of roles, turning the situation he had thought existed on its head in the space of a minute, had left him floundering, unsure of himself in a way that he hadn't been in a very long time.

That 'Well, hi,' was all that he could manage.

And 'Hi,' was all that she said right back, in a strangely similar tone.

He opened his arms to her, feeling that he was also opening his heart, exposing it, raw and vulnerable, so that it would tear him apart if she turned away now.

But she didn't. Instead, she came straight to him, like a bird flying home to its roost, and he enfolded her in his hug, holding her close and vowing to himself that he would never, ever let her go.

The water pounded down on them, too hard, too fierce for the way he was now feeling, and so he reached up one hand and switched it off with a snap, shaking the wetness from his saturated hair and sighing in relief as it eased, stilled, stopped.

'Cassandra...'

Her name was just a thick mutter against her mouth, a feeble attempt at the speech he felt incapable of making. Already his body was throbbing in urgent demand—and yet, strangely, the urgency was not for instant and rapid appeasement.

He needed something *more*. Something slower, longer, deeper.

More.

He needed something more emotionally satisfying.

And so he held her close, hugging her even tighter, lifting her from her feet and half carrying, half walking her from the shower stall, pushing the door aside until it banged against the wall.

'Joaquin…'

He couldn't tell if her use of his name was a question, a sound of agreement, or simply just another sigh. But she was limp and acquiescent in his arms, seemingly willing to go anywhere, any time with him. And so he carried her into the bedroom, snagging up a couple of thick white towels as he went.

Only when he reached the bed did he set her down, spreading out one of the towels, one-handed, on the deep blue coverlet before lowering her gently onto its softness. Then, taking the other towel and bending over her, he began to dry her water-dappled body.

Each stroke of the soft cotton was a caress. Each movement over the pink-tinted skin was followed by the touch of his lips, pressing against the warmly yielding flesh. Each kiss was accompanied by a murmured comment, a compliment crooned softly in his native Catalan, the language he lapsed into at the most intimate moments.

He told her how beautiful he found her. Whispered of the longings she lit in him, the hunger that burned away his soul. And in his mind he murmured secret words from his heart that even now he did not dare to let into the open for fear that they were not what she wanted to hear. That revealing them would risk making them shrivel into ashes as they left his mouth.

Her sighs answered him. Her body too responded mutely, stretching and twisting on the bed, her hair splayed out on the white towelling that cushioned her head. In the delicate blue veins he could feel her pulse beat strong and hard, and he heard her breathing quicken, rasping faintly in and out of her lungs.

Her hands were reaching for him now, pulling him up so that their mouths met in the deepest, longest, most satisfying kiss he had ever known.

'Cassandra!' he gasped, struggling for breath. '*Querida—belleza!* Do you know what you do to me—how you—?'

He broke off on a choking cry as those wickedly knowing slender hands closed about him intimately, stroking provocatively along the achingly hard length of his erection.

'Cassie!'

It was all that he could manage, the full syllables of her name beyond him. His tongue wouldn't form it; his breath couldn't last until he had completed it all. And besides, that 'Cassandra' suddenly seemed so wrong, so inappropriate to the moment.

And so, 'Cassie,' he sighed again, taking her mouth once more.

He had wanted her warm and willing and she was all that. Everything he could ever have dreamed of—and more. She was hungry for him, urgently pressing him onwards when he would have taken things even more slowly, taking the time to arouse and tantalise her even more, prolonging the waiting, the anticipation, and so heightening the pleasure to its peak for both of them.

Yet at the same time there was an unknown, a unique vulnerability about his woman tonight. And that new sensitivity seemed to communicate itself to him. It was as if it were the first time they had made love together—the first time he had *ever* made love in all his life. But at the same time there was a deep, powerful knowledge at the heart of it, a sense of experiences in the past, of lovers known and weighed against this one intense and powerful moment.

Weighed and found wanting. So damn wanting.

Every sense was heightened; every pleasure greater than ever before. The texture of her skin was the softest he had ever known, the scent of it pure intoxication. Her kisses were honey mixed with spice and her voice was husky music in his ears.

He had never felt so hard, so hot, so powerfully aroused, but at the same time he had never wanted to take things as slowly as he did this time. This time he wanted to indulge every sense, stretch out the pleasure to the highest peak, extend it to the longest possible time. He wanted to enjoy every heightened second, experience every hungry passion for as long as it could possibly endure.

Cassandra seemed to match his needs exactly. With an instinct that was uncannily close to mind-reading she recognised his desires almost before he knew them himself and for each pleasure he gave her she gave him back a hundredfold, feeding each sense, stirring new hungers, satisfying and enticing all in one wonderful moment.

'Joaquin,' she sighed against his kiss. 'I've wanted— needed...for so long. So long.'

'And I have too,' he assured her, knowing exactly how she felt.

It had been the longest week of his life. Seeming so much, so very much longer than a mere seven days. He felt as if he had been without her for ever. As if this had been their first magical time together. As if it had never been like this before.

'I've missed you, *querida*,' he muttered, the words harsh and rough from restraint in his throat. 'Missed you so much...'

His voice faded as he felt a tug inside his mind. Something that whispered of memory. Of a door opening briefly, just for a moment, and just enough to let a tiny sliver of light in before it drifted shut again and he was back in the present.

'I don't know how I waited...'

'Neither do I.' It came with a tiny bubble of laughter in her throat. 'Neither do I.'

'There were times when I thought I would die if I didn't have you back in my bed again. Die or go completely insane.'

'I know. I know. I felt that way too. So now...'

She shifted slightly, rubbing her slender body against his, her breasts brushing against his chest, her pelvis arching towards the heated hardness of his, long, pale legs tangling with his bronzed, hair-hazed limbs, making him groan aloud in yearning response.

'Don't wait any longer, Joaquin,' she whispered against his ear, trailing the warm dampness of her tongue around its curling edge, flicking teasingly against the softness of the lobe. 'Don't make me wait any longer—don't make *us* wait any longer.'

How could he wait any longer when she urged him on in that soft, persuasive voice? How could he deny her anything? How could he deny himself?

He pulled her underneath him and she moved easily, willingly, opening to him without any need of further encouragement. When he covered her body with his, feeling her fine strength supporting him, her softness cushioning him, it felt like coming home after the longest journey of his life.

He almost lost it then.

'Dios en el cielo!' he muttered through gritted teeth, struggling to control himself long enough to make this right, make it perfect for her.

He didn't know what was driving him that way, and why it mattered so damn much right now, at this time. There was some deep and cloudy memory lurking at the back of his mind, but one he couldn't pin down. And he didn't even want to try. He only knew that it *had* to be right. That he couldn't live with himself if he spoiled it now.

He sank into the moist, enveloping warmth of her as if

into liquid sunshine, bathing himself in it up to the hilt, pushing as far and as deep and as fully as he could. As strongly as he could.

And he held on for as long as he could, though it damn nearly killed him as Cassandra writhed and moaned beneath him, abandoning herself totally to sensation. Her delicate hands wreaked devastation on his self-control, touching in just the right places, tantalising, tormenting, driving him to distraction and beyond.

It was when she gave the small choking cry that he recognised of old, and her whole body tensed, that he knew his ordeal of waiting was almost at an end. A couple of frantic, ragged heartbeats later that cry became a moan, the moan a high, soaring sound of delight, and she arched underneath him, eyes tight shut, barely breathing as she lost herself in a wild and powerful climax.

He held her tighter than ever. Clasped her hard to him while the storm took her and her body shuddered against him again and again and again. And it was only when the peak of ecstasy began to subside that he let go of the reins on his own starving passion and followed her into the wild abyss of fulfilment.

Cassie came back to herself slowly and with difficulty. She woke to reality again to find herself with tears on her cheeks and a whirling confusion in the scrambled remains of her mind.

What had happened to her?

What had happened to *them*?

She and Joaquin had made love—slept together—hundreds of times over the past year and it had never, ever been like *this*.

Caught off guard, weak and foolishly vulnerable, totally lost in a world she didn't recognise, she could only focus on one thing. And it was something that terrified her.

This time it had felt like making love.

At any other time, under any other circumstances, she would have welcomed that fact. But tonight, right here and now, she didn't dare to let the thoughts slide into her mind.

Even if tonight something had happened to change Joaquin's way of thinking. Even if right now he felt something totally different from the hard and hungry passion that was all he had felt for her before. Even if her dream had actually come true and he was finally coming to care for her in the way that she had so longed for, she would be foolish, ridiculously blind, naïve and gullible, to think that she could rely on those feelings lasting.

Because they were based on a lie—or, if not a lie, then at least on a lack of any real understanding. Those four weeks that were missing from his memory must always come between them. And if Joaquin thought that he was feeling something different—something *more*—then, although it tore at her heart not to do so, she knew she could never, ever let herself trust those feelings.

When he remembered, it could destroy anything he felt now. It would certainly undermine the foundations of the things he thought he was experiencing. Because of that she could never let herself trust in it or believe in it or find any grounds at all for a hope of the future.

A tiny, single tear seeped out of the corner of one eye and slid slowly down onto her cheek, heading for her temple.

'Tears, *querida*?' a low, husky voice startled her by sounding from so very close by, and a second later Joaquin's warm lips were kissing away the tiny salty drop, his tongue taking it delicately into his own mouth.

Cassie's eyes flew wide open, stunned, wary blue eyes locking sharply with watchful black.

'Why tears, *belleza*? And why now?' he murmured. 'I can only hope that they are tears of joy—of fulfilment—of delight.'

'F-fulfilment, yes...' Cassie managed, her voice revealingly weak.

Some of them at least had been tears of delight. The tears she had shed at the highest point of her explosive orgasm. The tears that had totally escaped from her control and tumbled out of her eyes without her even being aware of it.

But that final, single tear hadn't been like that. It had been a sign of fear, of loss, of despair. A despair so overwhelming that she didn't even dare to face it in her own thoughts right now, let alone express it to him in any way.

But Joaquin didn't actually appear to be listening. Instead his attention was fixed on tracing the contours of her face with a long, gentle forefinger, his expression absorbed, his mind preoccupied.

'We were going to eat,' he murmured, his tone soft and richly sensual. 'But we seem to have got—distracted. Perhaps we should think about food now, hmm? Before the night is totally over.'

'I—I'm not hungry,' Cassie managed.

She didn't think she would ever eat again. She wouldn't need to. Not if they could stay here, like this, in the peaceful, dreamy aftermath of their passion, and never have to move, to think, to explain anything ever again.

But it seemed that Joaquin *was* hungry. Or at least restless. Dropping a slow, lingering kiss on her sleep-softened mouth, he pushed himself up and away from her, getting out of the bed and onto his feet, dark eyes looking round the room, searching for something.

He found it instantly, and with a small sound of satisfaction snatched up the pair of black pyjama bottoms that lay on a chair, pulling them on swiftly and silently.

'Joaquin?'

Cassie struggled to wake up properly, to pull herself from the drowsy, almost drugged weariness that the tumultuous climax had thrown her into at the end of their lovemaking. Even her eyes wouldn't focus fully and the long, lean shape of him was faintly blurred, the expression on his harshly carved face impossible to interpret.

'What...?'

But he waved an autocratic hand at her in a gesture demanding silence, turning even as he did so and striding swiftly out of the room.

She heard him head for the bedroom in which she had spent the long, lonely nights of the past week, and tensed instinctively, wondering just what he was doing.

How had she left her room? Was everything she had brought back from Ramón's unpacked and put away, making it look as if it had been there all the time—as if she had never been away? She knew that discovery must inevitably come some time soon, but, please, she begged whatever fate was watching over her, please not just now. Not just yet. If she could have this one special night unspoiled, undamaged by jealousy and suspicion, then it would serve as a memory to cling to when everything else might be destroyed and gone.

She didn't have time to worry for long. Only a moment or two later, Joaquin was back, and what he held in his hand made her heart lurch in sudden panicked remembrance.

'Here, put this on.'

He held out the pale green robe, the delicate silk looking impossibly flimsy when hanging from the tanned strength of his long fingers. Did he really not remember the last time he had seen her wearing it, the assumptions he had jumped to that night in Ramón's apartment?

He might not remember but she could not forget and the appalling accusations he had flung at her still echoed inside her head, etched into her thoughts in horror.

'Put it on?' she echoed warily, her thoughts filling with fearful images of him seeing her in the robe for the first time since the night of his accident. Of the sight reviving memories, of the inevitable explosion that would follow. She shivered convulsively inside. 'Why?'

But Joaquin ignored her hesitant question, instead reaching for her, lifting one arm and sliding the pale silk along it. He did the same with the other arm, then hoisted her up and out of the bed, pulling the robe around her body, smoothing it down, and then fastening the tie belt securely at her waist. His touch was firm and confident but strangely impersonal, every trace of the blazing sensuality of just moments before vanishing totally, his eyes hooded and dark, hiding the truth of his thoughts from her.

'There,' he said on a note of satisfaction. 'Now come with me.'

'But...'

Cassie tried a protest then gave it up on a secret shrug of resignation, knowing that to take it any further was to risk arousing his suspicions and making him wonder just why she was so uneasy. There had been no sign of any sort of recognition or remembrance on his handsome face as he had helped her into the robe, no hint that, like her, he was recalling painfully the last time he had seen her wearing it.

'Are we—do you plan to get something to eat?'

He didn't reply, but, taking her hand, led her firmly out onto the landing and down the stairs. And this time Cassie went along without any argument. Perhaps it was hunger that had set her stomach lurching queasily, making her feel nauseous and unwell as she had before. It was either that or an uncomfortable conscience combining with fearful apprehension at the thought of Joaquin's memory coming back.

Either way, she would feel better with some food inside her. Now that she remembered, she hadn't had anything since breakfast and then she'd only picked at a slice of toast. Not enough to give her the strength to get through to the late evening, which it now was.

But Joaquin didn't stop in the kitchen as she had expected. Instead, he led her through the quiet darkness of the living room, through the big patio doors, and out onto the terrace where the water of the swimming pool lapped gently against the sides, lit softly by the brightness of the moonlight.

'Joaquin?'

Her footsteps slowed, she pulled back on his hand, unsure of just what was happening.

'What is it? Where are we going?'

In her already unsettled state, it seemed as if the strongest shaft of moonlight came straight down onto the far side of the pool, illuminating as if in a spotlight the wooden lounger that stood there.

The wooden lounger on which she and Joaquin had made love the night before she had left him. Or tried to leave him. She had found it so terribly, terribly hard to leave him then, but this time it would cost her heart even more. This time she had known the sensation—or delusion, she didn't know which it was—of *really* making love with the man she adored. And because of that it was going to tear her heart in two if he ever remembered—and told her to get out of his life as a result.

Joaquin turned his dark head and smiled at her, the darkness of his eyes gleaming eerily in the moonlight.

'Wait and see,' he commanded. 'You'll find out soon enough.'

'But...'

To her horror he was leading her round the edge of the pool, heading—oh, dear heaven, was he heading for that lounger?

'Joaquin,' she managed again, struggling to make her voice sound natural. 'I—I'm not dressed for outdoors—I have hardly any clothes on.'

'You shouldn't let that worry you. I like you best with hardly any clothes on. And we're as private here as in the bedroom.'

Cassie's heart lurched painfully, thudding against her ribs so that it was difficult to breathe.

Did he know? Had he realised just how closely the words he was using had echoed the words he had used on that night they had been out here together, the night they had made love out in the open?

Or—worse—was it all quite deliberate?

Her legs felt disturbingly unsteady beneath her so that she stumbled on the tiled surround of the pool.

What if Joaquin had actually remembered? What if the lost traces of those few weeks had come back to him in their entirety and he was about to tell her so? And he was using the echoes of that night to give her warning of what was coming?

CHAPTER ELEVEN

PLEASE, no! It couldn't be that!

Cassie couldn't bear it if anguish came so soon after the wonderful way he had just made love to her. If he threw it all in her face and told her that he never wanted to see her again.

She couldn't go through it.

'No!'

The way Joaquin whirled round, his movement sharply abrupt, his face set into an expression of shock, told her that she had revealed too much. Her voice had given away all the panic that was building up inside her, and she had alerted him only too clearly to her precarious state of mind.

'No?' he questioned sharply, the edge on the single syllable chilling her blood in spite of the warmth of the night. 'Why no, *querida*? What is wrong?'

'I—I can't.'

'Can't what?'

'Can't—can't do this.'

His expression had stiffened even more, those dark pools of eyes watching her, suspicion stamped onto every hard line of his face. He still held her hand, but she could feel the difference in his grasp, the tightness that spoke of rigid control, of the determination to impose his will on the situation.

'Cassie…'

The warning note she dreaded was back, making the pronunciation of her name worryingly ominous.

'Just what is it that you cannot do? What are you afraid of?'

Oh, how did she answer that? A sudden high-pitched

sound, the flurry of wings, and a swirl of tiny dark forms
in the air gave her an answer that she grabbed at desperately.

'The bats!'

She sounded shaken enough to be genuine and as one of
the small night flyers came close she flinched away convincingly.

'I don't like the bats—they—'

'They're nothing to be afraid of!' Joaquin put in swiftly
and to her relief she realised that the faint shake in his voice
was put there by laughter, the anger and impatience reced-
ing slightly.

'Not for you perhaps! But I hate the way they fly around
your head—and they squeak!'

'They squeak!'

Now Joaquin was laughing openly, his head thrown
back, his strong features wonderfully relaxed in a way that
helped to ease the desperate racing of her heart.

'And that is what worries you? They will do you no
harm, *belleza*. None at all. As a matter of fact when I was
a small boy I once tried to capture one to keep as a pet.'

'You did?'

Intrigued by the image and by the thought of him as a
young child, Cassie turned fascinated eyes on his shadowed
face.

'Did you succeed?'

Joaquin nodded briefly, his laughter easing.

'But I only kept it for a day or so. I had forgotten that
bats are nocturnal—Señora did nothing at all in the light,
and I was asleep when she wanted to be active.'

'Señora? Is that what you called it?'

'Señora Murciélago. Dame Bat, if you like. To tell you
the truth, I wasn't even sure if she was a she—but I thought
she might be. She was cute. So you see, you have chosen
the perfect man.'

'I have?'

The abrupt transition from laughter to sober-faced gravity was disturbing, making her nerves tighten painfully again.

'For what?'

To protect you from bats—for the rest of your life if you'll let me. Cassandra…'

He was even more serious now, his expression sombre and intent, deep-set eyes searching her face.

'No,' she said fearfully, sensing what was coming, and dreading it. 'No, please.'

But Joaquin ignored her, his touch on her hand gentling again as he drew her close, bringing her up against his chest. His hand came under her chin, lifted her face to his, black eyes burning into blue as he looked down at her.

'Marry me, Cassandra,' he said softly. 'Marry me and I promise I'll keep you safe from all the bats—safe from anything—everything. I promise.'

Safe. The word seemed to form a tight knot in her throat, closing it off, threatening to choke her.

He would keep her safe from anything—from everything—but he couldn't keep her safe from himself.

'But—but you said that you don't d-do marriage…'

Oh, how she wished he would look away. Wished that that searing dark gaze would look anywhere but into her face where she was sure that all her fears and her doubts, all her secrets, must be openly etched for him to read.

'You don't do commitment,' she whispered, low and desperate. 'N-no ties.'

'I said that, but I wasn't thinking straight at the time.'

'And—and you are now? Thinking straight?'

But of course he couldn't be. How could he be thinking straight when he didn't have all the facts at his disposal? How could he know what he felt when he didn't know what had happened, what he had believed so totally about her? How could he ask her to marry him when he didn't even really know who she was any more?

'I think I am.'

He sounded so confident. But he couldn't be. And she couldn't trust a word he was saying until the truth was out.

The stunning masculine face before her blurred terribly and the bitter sting of salt was in the tears that were pushing at the back of her eyes. But she couldn't let them fall, even though she had to bite her lip hard against the need to abandon herself to them, using the small pain to hold back the misery that she felt inside.

'I believe I've never thought straighter in my whole life. That it's only now that I know what I want—what I truly want.'

'And—' She could hardly catch her breath enough to say it. 'And that is?'

'Oh, Cassandra, *querida*, you know—what I want is *you*.'

Taking her hand again, he led her to the wooden lounger and sank down onto it, drawing her down after him. Side by side on the padded cushions, he held both her hands in his, once more looking deep and fixedly into her clouded, troubled eyes.

'Let me tell you something about my family. About my father—and Ramón and Alex.'

Cassie could only nod in silence and wait for him to speak. She had never quite been able to work out the complicated relationships that made up Joaquin's family tree.

'You know that both my brothers are really only half-brothers—that we all have the same father, but different mothers? I was just fifteen when I found out about Ramón—when I learned that my father had been unfaithful to my mother. That he had fathered another child with a lover he had been seeing almost from the beginning of his marriage. And then, some years later, Alex too turned up— another son—another woman as his mother. Another infidelity.'

Shaking his dark head, he looked away from her, staring

out at the water in the pool, his eyes seeming glazed and unfocused in the moonlight.

'I thought they had the perfect marriage. I couldn't have been more wrong. It was just an arranged union—no love, no commitment in it. Nothing but a dynastic arrangement, with a financial bonus thrown in. My father had never meant to stay true to his marriage vows. And I was his son. So like him, everyone said. So very like him.'

'But not in your career,' Cassie had to put in. 'You never wanted to work in the media—you always dreamed of setting up your own vineyard, developing the wines.'

'*El Loco?*'

Joaquin's mouth twisted up slightly at one side in an expression of cynical amusement.

'And that's the only way we're different—but in the way I wanted to be unlike him, I was so damn similar. Like father, like son—and I was his son in every other way, or so I thought. I thought I could never be happy with just one woman. That like him I was meant to play the field, a new relationship every year—a new woman in my bed.'

White teeth digging into her bottom lip again, Cassie ducked her head to hide the sheen of tears that she knew was making her eyes glisten betrayingly. Joaquin was telling her nothing she didn't already know. And he was explaining it much more gently than he had done before, when he had thrown that 'no ties, no commitment' speech right in her face. But, in spite of that gentleness, this time it hurt even worse than before. Because this time she knew that he was telling her nothing but the truth.

'I understand,' she sighed and was stunned when he caught at her shoulders, shaking her almost roughly in an attempt to drive his message home to her.

'No, you don't, *belleza*—you can't!' he told her harshly. 'You wouldn't use that tone if you knew what I was really trying to say. What I truly want you to know.'

'I don't?'

Cassie's head came up, blue eyes dazed-looking under the frown of confusion that drew her fair brows together.

'I can't—what do you want me to know?'

'That I've realised that I'm not like my father. That I no longer want to drift from woman to woman, from one relationship to another. I've changed. I need you to believe that. And I want you to have this…'

Reaching into his pocket, he pulled out a small dark blue box. When he flicked it open the brilliant, perfect solitaire gleamed wonderfully in the light of the moon, and it was so beautiful that Cassie felt as if her heart had stopped simply at the sight of it. And when her pulse started up again, making her breathe once more, it went rocketing along her veins, racing wildly all over her body.

'Joaquin…' she croaked, but her voice died on her, leaving her incapable of managing another word.

'Marry me, Cassandra,' Joaquin went on, his voice raw and husky in a way she had never heard before. 'Say you'll accept my proposal—that you'll let me be with you for ever. And believe that I mean it.'

'I believe you.'

The terrifying thing was that she *did* believe him. That there was no room for doubt in her mind when she looked into the sombre cast of his face, into the burning depths of his eyes. Joaquin meant this. He meant every word of it. At least as much of it as he could believe without knowing what had happened between them.

Perhaps if she hadn't been sitting here, on this lounger where they had been that night, perhaps if she hadn't been wearing the robe that he had taken as part evidence against her when he had come to Ramón's flat, then she might have been able to cope with this. Might even have allowed herself to hope. But the terrible, the heart-wrenchingly bitter irony was the fact that now, at last, when the man she loved had finally proposed to her in a way that she could believe, a way that should have made her heart sing with joy, instead it dropped her spirits right down to their lowest possible ebb, draining all the life, all the hope of happiness from her.

'Then say yes,' Joaquin urged. 'Say you'll marry me.'

'I don't—I...'

'You must have known that this was coming. Must have understood that you were different—that you were special to me.'

'Must I?'

'But of course!'

Joaquin dismissed the question as if it was the most ridiculous thing imaginable.

'You know how long we've been together—that you're the only woman I've ever stayed with longer than a year.'

Longer than a year!

Cassie almost broke down at the savage pain of it, wanting to wrap her arms around her trembling body to hold herself together, stop herself from falling apart. The nausea that had troubled her before was back in full force and she felt weak and shaken, all her strength seeming to have seeped away in the time they had been outside.

Technically, she supposed it was true. They had been together for more than the year that Joaquin normally allowed his relationships to last. But they had only Joaquin's loss of memory to thank for that. Without it, they would have separated and gone their different ways more than two weeks ago. And when those missing days resurfaced in Joaquin's mind, he was going to know that too and deeply regret the impetuous proposal he had just made.

'So what's your answer?'

'I—you see—I—no! No, I can't! No, I won't! I won't marry you. Please don't ask me! I won't—Joaquin, the answer is *no*!'

No?

It was the last thing he had been expecting. It exploded

in his face like a land-mine, blasting his thoughts into oblivion, leaving him incapable of focusing on anything.

Anything except that one, appalling, unwanted, hateful word.

'*No?*' he said, his voice not sounding like his own. 'No! You don't mean that!'

'I do,' Cassie returned, but there was no conviction in her voice, nothing that made him believe her totally. At least not enough to give up.

'I won't accept it.'

'Oh, please! You must! You have to!'

The look on her pale face pleaded with him to believe her, but he was in no mood to take what she was saying.

'Have to?' he echoed savagely, hating the phrase. 'Have to—and tell me, *querida*, why the hell do I *have* to accept this?'

'Because of your accident—you said you were thinking straight but you can't possibly be. You can't really know what you feel. You might regret this when your memory comes back.'

'Never! I am telling you that I love you. How can I ever regret that? Cassandra, I don't care about my memory of those four weeks—'

Were those tears in her eyes or just the reflection of the moonlight? Tears were good—if they meant that she was weakening. That she might reconsider. But the next moment took his hopes and dashed them to the ground.

'But I do. I have to. I can't marry you. You have to take my answer, Joaquin—it's the only one I can give you for now.'

For now.

He pounced on the words. 'For now' sounded more hopeful. It sounded like a reprieve, holding the door open just a tiny crack.

'I shall ask you again,' he told her. 'Some day my damn

memory must come back, and when it does I'll ask you again to be my wife.'

It was supposed to make her feel better. To show her that he really was serious about this. That he meant every word he had said. But somehow it seemed to have exactly the opposite effect. If it was possible, her pale skin lost even more colour so that it appeared almost translucent and her eyes seemed dulled and dazed.

'All right, then,' she said softly, wearily. 'I'll go along with that. When your memory comes back, if you still want to ask me again, then I promise I'll listen.'

It wasn't all he had dreamed of. But it was as much as he could hope for. And he would have to be satisfied with it. For now at least.

'I'll hold you to that,' he said harshly, struggling to keep his already uncertain grip on his feelings. 'This isn't going to go away, Cassandra. I won't let it.'

He ran a finger along the lines of shadow under her eyes, noting the look of exhaustion on her face.

'But tonight you're tired—we both are. We'll see how things look after a good night's sleep.'

Getting to his feet, he drew her up with him, one arm around her waist, holding her tight so that she couldn't break away from him if she tried.

'But we sleep in the same bed,' he told her, his tone making it clear that there was no way he was going to concede this point, no matter how she argued. 'I don't give a damn about any doctors and their orders, or anything else. I want you with me, beside me, in my bed—where you belong.'

She didn't argue. For a second he thought she might. She opened her mouth, drew a breath, seemed to think of it. But then in the space of the same heartbeat she changed her mind, swallowed down what she had been about to say, and closed her eyes, nodding silently in surrender.

'Good,' was all he said as he swung her up into his arms,

supporting her head against his shoulder, her slender body against his chest. She was his woman, and one day she would see that was true.

His woman. He felt his heart lift and a new warmth of joy creep into it as if he were bathed in the warmth of the morning sun, not the cool, pale light of the moon.

She would spend the night in his bed, sleep in his arms, they would wake up together tomorrow.

And tomorrow was another day.

Another day when he would start his campaign afresh, and one day, some day, she would give him the answer he wanted.

He wasn't prepared to take that 'No' she had given him. There was no way he could live with that.

So he took her to his bed, and it was just as he had imagined. For all that she was so tired, Cassandra turned to him and held him close, and once more the inevitable passion flared between them, hot and strong and undeniable. The long hours of the night were burned away in that passion, taking all time, all memory, all uncertainty with them so that there was no room for anything else. No space in his mind for anything but the knowledge that this was the woman he wanted for the rest of his life.

He fell asleep on that thought. Replete and contented, and totally sure that tonight had just been a temporary glitch, an unexpected twist on the path towards the future he had believed was in his grasp. He slept deeply and long, barely even registering the vivid dreams that filled what little was left of the night, waking when the sun was high in the sky, and the time on the clock told him that he was late. That unless he went *now*, he would miss the meeting completely.

Automatic pilot got him out of bed and into the shower when it was the last thing he wanted. The same unthinking instinct made sure he was dressed and ready, forcing down the furious protests of the body that longed to be back in the bed beside Cassandra, and the heart that was in total agreement with that need.

He wanted to lie with her in his arms and watch her slowly emerge from the deep, exhausted sleep she had fallen into. He wanted to inhale the sweet scent of her skin, kiss her awake with the taste of her on his lips. He wanted to hear her soft sigh, see her eyelids flutter open, her eyes looking straight into his as she came back to reality. Most of all he wanted to see their clear, bright blue darken and cloud with the desire for him that there was no way she could hide.

But because of this stupid, boring meeting there was no way he could do that now. Cursing the fact that he hadn't deputised someone to stand in for him, he tried to head for the door, only to know as his hand touched the door that he couldn't make himself go now.

Not yet. Not without a word of goodbye; without one last kiss; without seeing Cassandra one last time.

He'd really got it bad, he told himself, shaking his head in despair at the way he was acting as he mounted the stairs. He really had lost his heart and his soul to this woman if just the thought of being away from her for a couple of hours did this to him.

It was as he came to the top of the stairs, turning to walk down the landing, that something, some trick of the light, some warning little voice hidden until now, some secret realisation jolted his thoughts and made him realise that something was wrong.

He wasn't thinking straight at all. He didn't have to go to work. He didn't have to go anywhere.

It was a Saturday. It was Saturday morning, and so it didn't matter how late he woke, how long he stayed in bed. The meeting with the London buyers that he had thought he had to go to wasn't an appointment he had to meet at all. It wasn't even happening today.

He was up and dressed, and on his way out—to a dinner that had actually been held three weeks before.

His footsteps stilled. The hand that he had raised to open the bedroom door froze in mid-air, the action uncompleted. And he knew what had happened.

The dreams that had pursued him through the night had taken his numbed brain and shaken it awake. The effects of the accident, of the blow to the head, had eased at last, sweeping away the clouds and leaving his thoughts as clear and sharp as they had ever been.

The lost month was missing no more. His memories were back, strong and vivid and totally devastating.

Because now that he could see those memories so starkly, he knew exactly why he had wanted to erase them from his thoughts.

CHAPTER TWELVE

CASSIE came awake slowly and reluctantly.

The deep, deep sleep into which she had fallen had held her like someone drugged and even now, with the sunlight bright enough to burn through her closed eyelids, she still wanted to stay exactly where she was. She longed to linger in this half-asleep half-waking state where nothing else mattered but her blissful contentment and the knowledge that Joaquin was there, beside her...

But he wasn't.

A faint frown creased the space between her eyebrows as the questing hand she had put out to find the man in whose arms she had fallen asleep encountered only empty space and the rapidly cooling sheets that told her Joaquin had left their bed some time before.

It was enough to bring back the memories. Images of the other time when she had woken late to find Joaquin gone flashed through her thoughts, jolting her wide awake in a shocking rush. Had he left her to sleep—or had he other things he planned to do, as he had that time? Or was she just making too much of a simple absence?

Oh, when would this constant fear of Joaquin's memory returning leave her? Or wasn't the truth that it never would? Because if he remembered everything then the fear would become so much worse—becoming a fear of reality, rather than anticipation.

The thought was enough to jolt her upright, sitting up in bed in sudden shock, and then wincing as the unguarded movement made her head spin unpleasantly.

Not enough to eat, she realised belatedly. They had never had that meal last night, which meant that she hadn't eaten solid food for over twenty-four hours. And a solid diet of stress and caffeine had done nothing to help her feel any better. In fact she felt...

'Oh, no!'

The thought of food had brought a wave of nausea, one that had her flinging back the bedclothes and dashing for the bathroom. She only just made it in time to lurch over the basin, retching and heaving miserably.

Oh, now what was wrong? Didn't she have enough on her plate without being ill? Or...

Horror held her frozen, unable to think, unable even to breathe. Was it...?

'Something you ate, *querida*?' A darkly cynical voice from behind finished the question that she didn't even dare to ask herself.

'I don't know,' she managed to mumble, keeping her head bent, her hair concealing her face, the panic she knew must show in her eyes.

She knew she must look at her least glamorous possible, in total disarray, with not a stitch of clothing to cover her, but an ice-cold shaft of fear cut away any embarrassment she might fear, leaving only a freezing, dark sense of horror. Something about Joaquin's tone warned her there was much worse to come and his next words confirmed as much.

'You don't know? I thought it was me that had the memory problems, not you. So tell me, *amada*, is it likely that this means what I suspect it does—and if that's the case then is the baby most likely to be mine or my brother's? Or is that something else you ''don't know''?'

So how did she answer that in a way that she could make him believe? Cassie's throat was already raw and uncomfortable from being sick, but now the drying effects of fear added to the sensation as she straightened up, drew in a deep, ragged breath, struggling to find the strength with which to answer him.

'You've remembered,' she croaked, her face still turned away, her hair in a tangled mess over her pallid face.

'I've remembered,' Joaquin confirmed icily. 'I've remembered everything—absolutely everything.'

'I'm glad.'

She was too, though it hurt her terribly to say it. The days of waiting, fearing, dreading this moment had stretched her nerves to breaking-point. She couldn't have taken much more if she'd tried. At least now, this way, the axe had fallen. She no longer had to wonder what would happen when it did.

She knew. And it was every bit as bad as she had feared.

In fact, it was worse, she added wretchedly as she finally found the strength to lift her head and look at Joaquin's reflection in the mirror. He was lounging in the bathroom doorway, strong arms folded across his chest, his stunning face set into harsh lines of rejection and cold fury. The same fury that turned his eyes opaque and impenetrable when they locked onto her own nervous gaze through the glass.

'Glad?' he echoed now, turning her word into a sound of pure contempt. 'How can you be glad when this means I've found you out, that I—'?

'I said I'm glad and I meant it!' Cassie flung out, whirling round to face him so fast that it made her head spin and she had to clutch at the white porcelain basin behind her for support. 'I'm glad that your memory's come back, glad that you no longer have to live with a hole in your life where those weeks should be—glad that—that...'

'That I remember what you've been up to?' Joaquin drawled, low and dangerously intent. 'That I now know— or at least have some suspicion just whose bastard you might have tried to foist on me.'

'Whose...?'

Through the dizzy buzzing inside her head, Cassie struggled hard to make sense of what he was saying. She didn't know yet if she was pregnant, though she had to admit it was a horrifying possibility, but Joaquin at least appeared convinced that she was. He also seemed to think that—

'That's just not true!' she gasped when realisation of just what he meant hit home to her beleaguered brain. 'I would never do that! And besides—'

'No?' Joaquin cut in again. 'So what have you been doing all week? Staying here with me while knowing all the time that you were pregnant with—'

'I knew nothing of the sort! I *didn't*!' she emphasised as a cynically lifted eyebrow questioned the truth of her declaration. 'I didn't know—or even suspect that I might be pregnant until now.'

'Naïve of you. After all, sexual activity is what makes a baby and, as you've been more active than most, you might at least have had some sort of suspicion.'

But that was just too much.

'How dare you? How dare you imply—? I have *not* been more sexually active than most...'

'Sleeping with two members of the same family at the same time doesn't count, then?' Joaquin enquired so nastily that her fingers itched to wipe the sneering contempt from his face with a well-aimed slap. She had to twist them together tightly in front of her to keep herself from giving in to that temptation.

'No, it doesn't, because I haven't done any such thing! I wouldn't!'

'No?'

'No! So you can take that damned sneer off your face— and if you were any sort of a gentleman you'd not stand there like that—you might at least have the courtesy to let me past and let me get dressed!'

She would feel just a little more at ease if she got dressed, she told herself. Not better. Nothing could make her feel better about this hateful situation—but she might at least feel a bit more comfortable, less shockingly vulnerable, if she was covered up.

'*Perdón lo siento!* I am deeply ashamed!' Joaquin flung back with a cynicism that made a total mockery of his claim to penitence, making her wince as if the lash of his tongue had been an actual physical flick of a whip. 'But somehow, when I am with you, there is something that makes me forget to behave like a gentleman.'

But all the same he moved away from the door, stepping back into the bedroom so that she could come past.

Struggling to preserve any tiny shreds of the dignity that had totally deserted her, Cassie forced herself to march past him, head held defiantly high, every ounce of strength she possessed exerted to keep her legs from wobbling, her face from revealing the misery that ravaged her soul.

She made it to the bed before her strength deserted her and she sank down on the edge of it, thankful that she hadn't actually fallen.

'Here…'

Joaquin's rough-spoken words drew her attention and, looking up, she was amazed to find that he was holding something out to her.

The green silk robe that she had been wearing the night before.

And that was something she couldn't put on. Something that came too interwoven with memories, good and bad, for her to wear with any degree of ease, or any hope of getting Joaquin to forget just why he was so furious with her.

'Oh, no,' she managed, shaking her head violently so that her hair swirled around her face, golden strands catching on her mouth, her eyelashes. 'No—please—don't you have anything else?'

'Like what?'

Following the direction of her wildly waving hand, he

dropped the silk to the floor and snatched up the item she had indicated, tossing it into her lap.

Cassie stared at the black cotton with a desolate, sinking feeling in her heart. Was the black cotton robe that she had worn in such similar circumstances on the morning before she had left Joaquin any better at all? she couldn't help wondering. Or was it in fact worse?

Because some cruel, malign fate had led to Joaquin putting on exactly the same sleek steel-coloured suit as he had worn that last morning before he had left for work. In fact his outfit was exactly the same, right down to the burgundy and blue tie, the gold cufflinks that gleamed at his wrists. It made her think of some sort of appalling action replay, going back over some of the worst moments of her life.

But at least the black robe was some sort of cover, some protection from those cruelly assessing eyes. That was something to be thankful for. So she huddled herself into its enveloping folds, hugging it tightly around her and cinching the belt in so hard that it dug into her flesh.

'Haven't we been here before?' Joaquin drawled cynically, jet-hard eyes flicking over her slim form with undisguised contempt. 'And I suspect the end this time will be much the same as the last—only this time I'll be the one to shut the door behind you when you walk.'

Was she hearing things, Cassie couldn't help wondering, or had there been a hint of extra bitterness in that last comment? The sort that, if she was even more weak and foolish than she was already, she might actually be fool enough to think had come from some deep inner feeling, some long-standing regret that he was trying to hide.

Oh, who was she trying to kid? Regret was not in Joaquin's vocabulary, nor was 'deep feeling', not unless she was very badly mistaken.

'You think I'm going to leave?'

Desperately needing something to do, Cassie's restless

fingers pleated the black cotton covering her knees over and over again.

'I *know* you're going to leave. I don't want you here in my home, in my life any longer. I want you to pack your bags and go. That was the very first thought that came into my head when I realised that I remembered—and what I remembered. So now are you still going to claim that you're glad my memory has come back?'

'Yes.'

It came out on a deep sigh.

'Yes, I'm still glad—I couldn't be anything else. At least, not for you.'

'Yeah, it's worked out fine for me.' Joaquin acceded, nodding his head, a cynical twist on his lips, a savage light in his eyes. 'But not so wonderfully for you. You should have grabbed at my marriage proposal while it was still on offer, Cassie, *querida*. You might have had a chance then. But at least I expect you still have Ramón as a stand-by option. If, of course, he still wants you when he knows you're back to sharing your favours between us.'

'You're completely wrong about Ramón, you know,' Cassie sighed despondently. 'He's not interested in me—never has been. He's lost his heart to a fiery Spanish lady who's been making his life a misery. The trouble is that he just doesn't know it yet.'

'Well, in that case you should have a chance to make your move before he realises. Get in there fast and he—'

'No,' Cassie cut in, cool and firm, not allowing him to finish the statement.

'No? Why not?'

'I should have thought that was obvious.'

She forced herself to her feet, relieved to find that her legs supported her much more steadily this time. At least the violence of the nausea was starting to ebb away a little, though the sight of her appearance in the mirror made her grimace in appalled distaste.

She looked dreadful with her face pale, her eyes red-rimmed and her hair like a windblown haystack. But she was past caring. All she could think about was the shocking things Joaquin believed her capable of, the bitterness they had caused him. And all she wanted to do was to get the truth home to him in whatever way she could.

But how?

'Why is it obvious?' Joaquin persisted, giving her the best cue she could ever want.

She brought her head up, chin lifting determinedly. And she looked him straight in the eyes so that he could be in no doubt at all that she meant what she said.

'I've no intention of making any move on Ramón for two reasons—one, because I know he's already involved with someone, and two, because there is only one Alcolar that I'm in the least bit interested in—and that's you.'

Only one Alcolar—and that's you.

If she had given him the slap that he knew her fingers had been itching to deliver just a few moments before, then she couldn't have knocked him back more strongly, Joaquin admitted to himself. Because the problem was that he almost caught himself believing her. Hell, he *wanted* to believe her, even though he knew he was being all kinds of a fool if he did so.

But he couldn't doubt the evidence of his own eyes. And he'd seen her, installed in Ramón's flat, in that damnably seductive slip of a gown, and she'd told him herself that his brother gave her something special.

'He gives me something that you never did!' were the words she had flung at him that night. The night when he'd had the accident, when all memory of the occasion had been wiped from his mind. And, using that, she had moved back in with him again, playing him like a fool, bringing him to the point where he had confessed his feelings for her. Hell, he'd even proposed again—a proper proposal of marriage this time, not like the desperate, wildly foolish one she'd forced from him in Ramón's apartment.

And what had she said then?

'My answer is no! No! Never! No way! Not in my lifetime! I wouldn't marry you if you were the last man alive on this earth and the future of the human race depended on it.'

She couldn't have made it clearer if she'd tried.

Oh, why the hell had he ever had to lose his memory? If only he could have remembered just how things had been then he would never, ever have let her back into his life. Never given her his heart to play with like a toy. Never had to stand there while she tossed it right back at him again, with yet another thoughtless refusal of his offer of marriage.

And now she expected him to believe this preposterous claim of 'only one Alcolar'.

His response to that was very curt, short, and obscene, making her eyes widen sharply.

'It's true!' she protested.

'Yeah—sure.'

He dismissed the words with a flick of his hand.

'Nice try, *amada*, but I really don't believe you! I'd be a fool to believe a single word that comes from that lovely lying little mouth of yours. I mean—you just spent the last week here in my home, pretending nothing had happened...'

'I *had* to! And you know why. I was acting on—'

'On doctors' orders!' Joaquin finished for her, bitterness lacing his tone with black. 'Yes, I know—I should do— you told me often enough. But wasn't it convenient that those wonderful doctors' orders should coincide so perfectly with exactly what suited you best—keeping me totally in the dark so that you could work out your own mercenary little scheme?'

Cassandra moved restlessly from one foot to another,

seemingly unable to keep still. She pushed her hands deep into the pockets of the robe, then pulled them out again, raked her fingers through her hair, apparently meaning to smooth it but in fact making the tangles so much worse. And had he been seeing things or had her hands had a distinct tremor as they'd moved?

'What scheme?'

'The one that kept you in my house, ostensibly looking after me—and winning my trust—when all the while you were after something else!'

That stopped her nervy fidgeting. It changed her mood too, in a startling way. Her jaw set firmly, her mouth stiffening, and she tossed back the long mane of blonde hair with a gesture of defiance.

'And just what was I after?'

Joaquin recognised with fury the immediate and unwanted way that his body responded to the new fire in her eyes, the flare of colour along her cheeks. That same colour was echoed behind the opening at the throat of the robe, tinting her neck, and the soft skin below it, the beginnings of the sweet curves of her breasts, with the rosy pink of her raised blood.

She looked strong and magnificent—all woman; a real woman—and that woman called to the most primitive part of his masculinity with a heady, feminine power that made his head swim. What he wanted most in all the world was to grab her and throw her down onto the bed, rip that enveloping robe from the glorious body and bury himself in her, forgetting all his determination to be strong, to face her with what she had done and get her out of his life.

It was all that he could do to clamp his hands into tight fists at his sides, digging his nails into his palms to keep himself thinking straight and not wandering off onto the paths of sensual temptation.

'Joaquin,' Cassandra persisted, her voice low and determined. 'Just what am I supposed to have been after when I came back here—other than to look after you, of course?'

'Isn't it obvious? You wanted a home—a rich man to care for you. You must have already begun to guess that you were *embarazada*—that you were having a child. And it must have been too early for it to be Ramón's, unless…'

'No!' She had seen the way his mind was working and jumped in swiftly to deny it. '*No!* There was no way it could have been Ramón's! Do you hear me? No way!'

'Well, then, you knew that my brother would realise the child was mine. While I didn't remember that you'd ever left me, ever run to be with my brother, you took your chance—you moved back in here with me, made sure that I could only believe that the child was mine, hoping that I would think I was the only man you'd ever slept with…'

'You *are* the only man I've slept with. Since I met you at least—there has been no one else in my life.'

She sounded too convincing. Too bloody believable. But the fiery rage inside his head was stopping him from thinking and he swept on, carried along on a tide of fury as hot and burning as the flood of lava from a newly erupted volcano.

'And you nearly got what you wanted. I was actually ready to make you my wife. You got a proposal of marriage out of me.'

'Which I refused.'

She'd scored a point there, Cassie thought with grim satisfaction. She'd actually stopped him dead, mid-flow, his black eyes going to her face, wide and shocked, the pupils so distended that they covered almost all the iris.

'What?'

He looked so stunned that she almost felt sorry for him. But she couldn't afford to back down now. For the first time since he had come up behind her in the bathroom, she felt as if the tide was actually turning in her favour. For the first time he seemed on the point of, if not backing down, at least acknowledging that she had some cause for justification. And she couldn't let that opportunity slip from her hands.

'Have you listened to yourself, Joaquin?' she asked. 'Have you? Have you looked at what you're claiming with any sort of rational thought—subjected it to a logical examination?'

His silence told her that she had his attention and so she pressed her advantage as hard as she could.

'You claim that I left you to go and live with Ramón, but then your accident forced me back here to look after you. And that fitted with my plans because I'd just discovered that I might be pregnant...'

Might be pregnant! The words rang in her head until she almost lost track of her train of thought. She'd never actually registered the real depth of meaning of them before. *Might be pregnant.* With Joaquin's baby, whether he believed it or not. Oh, Lord, what was she going to do if this was right?

'That's what I said.' Joaquin's words dragged her from the confusion in her head, forcing her to focus once again. 'Then tell me this—if that's the way I was thinking, then why did I turn down your proposal of marriage last night? Why didn't I just snatch that ring from your hand and cram it on my finger just as soon as I possibly could?'

His stunned silence spoke more eloquently of his feelings than any words could do. But she could still see an argument forming in his thoughts, the storm clouds gathering in his eyes, and she hurried to reinforce her argument.

'I couldn't say yes, can't you see that? I loved you too much...'

'Love!' It was a short, hard, cynical laugh, breaking into her words and shattering the train of her point. '*Love!* Oh, now you're really pushing things. I can't believe that!'

'Why not?'

To her astonishment, Cassie suddenly felt totally calm.

And it wasn't the numbed calm of desperation. Instead she had never felt sharper or clearer in her life. It was the thought that she might be pregnant that had done this to her. The thought that she was fighting, not just for herself, but also for her baby's future. Her child would need a father—and Joaquin too would need his baby, even if he didn't see that right at this moment.

'Why don't you believe I love you? After all, if I didn't care for you then it would have been the easiest thing in the world to say yes, I'll marry you. To force you to commit right there and then even though I knew you weren't ready to make that decision.'

'I was!' Joaquin growled savagely. 'I knew what I was saying—what I wanted.'

'I know—and I believed you then. But I knew that you weren't thinking with a clear mind, that there were things you couldn't know—things I'd had to keep from you. And I believed so much that you meant it that I couldn't say yes, even if it was what I wanted most in all the world. I couldn't say yes because it would be taking advantage of the difficult position your loss of memory had put you in. I knew you might come to regret what you said—and I was right about that, wasn't I?'

She felt as if her heart had stopped beating, as if her breathing were totally suspended, as she waited for his answer.

'Wasn't I?'

Her answer was there in his face. She watched it change; knew her fate before he began to speak. And her heart broke deep inside as she heard his words confirm her thoughts.

'Yes,' he said, slowly and starkly. 'Yes, I regretted my proposal. I regretted it like hell.'

That was her dismissal, Cassie knew. There was nothing more she could say or do. She could only turn and go. Leave with some dignity at least.

'I thought so,' she said sadly, too low, too desolate even for tears. Her eyes were dry and aching and she had to clench her fists in order to keep herself from rubbing at them savagely. 'I'll go and pack.'

She managed three steps towards the door, her heart aching even more savagely with each movement she made. One foot in front of another, and then again—and still Joaquin stood there, stony eyes, stony-faced, just watching.

One more step.

She reached out for the door.

'No!'

It came so suddenly, so loudly, that she actually jumped inches off the floor, somehow landing facing back the way she had come so that she could see the change that had come over his face, the drained, shattered expression that had etched deep lines and white marks around the blazing eyes, the tightly drawn mouth.

'No,' he said again, more quietly but none the less steadily this time. 'I can't—I can't let you go. I can't let you walk out on me again. I barely survived the last time. I can't go through that again.'

'You…?' Cassie tried, unable to believe what she was hearing. 'You…'

But Joaquin wasn't listening. He didn't wait for her to struggle to get out the question that was on her lips. The question that was the most important thing she had ever had to ask in the whole world and yet somehow couldn't find a single word to express in any way.

Instead, he came straight to her side, taking her hand in his and holding it so tightly that it seemed he feared she would break free, run from him, escape.

Not that Cassie was capable of any such thing. Her legs had never felt so weak, and her whole body was trembling with shock. The burn of emotion in Joaquin's deep, dark eyes had quite shattered her, leaving her confused and bewildered and not knowing which way to turn.

Then he made matters so much worse by going down on one knee right there on the carpet before her. She couldn't believe what she was seeing, but, still clasping her hand, he looked up into her face, his gaze holding hers transfixed, unable to look away.

'Cassandra, I was talking nonsense—total garbage! I was hurt and angry and in shock and I've said the stupidest things and I don't mean a single one of them. I'm going to try again,' he said, and if she hadn't already been shocked into stillness then the note in his voice would have knocked her for six in a split second. It was rough and husky, raw with the sort of emotion she had never heard from him before. And it was utterly, totally compelling.

'T-try what again?' she stumbled, needing to speak but not knowing at all what to say.

'I've proposed marriage to you twice already and each time, I've made a total mess of it. The first time—at Ramón's was an insult, but it was also a cry of desperation. I'd have done anything, anything at all, to get you to come back to me. And I thought you wanted marriage, so that was what I offered—I even had the ring in my pocket, though I made it sound like the worst possible sort of life sentence at the time.'

With his free hand he pushed back the lock of black silky hair that had fallen over his forehead, his eyes not leaving hers for a second.

'I was in shock—I didn't know what I was saying. I'd been going crazy since you left me. I looked everywhere for you but I couldn't find you anywhere. And then suddenly there you were—with Ramón.'

'In Ramón's apartment,' Cassie put in gently. She didn't want to distract him from what he was about to say, but she couldn't let him persist in that illusion. 'I was staying at Ramón's, but I wasn't living *with* him.'

'I know.' Joaquin's expression was shamefaced and he shook his head in despair at his own stupidity. 'Deep down inside, I always knew, but I wasn't thinking straight—I wasn't thinking at all. I'd seen you and Ramón together and—well, I'll admit, I've always had something of a problem where my brother is concerned. He was everything my father wanted—and I was fool enough to think that perhaps he was what you wanted too.'

'How could he be?' Cassie questioned softly. 'When all I want is you? I told you, there's only one Alcolar that I love. And you're that man.'

'Then why…?'

She saw the shadows on his face, the pain of memory that clouded his eyes, and guessed intuitively at the question he was going to ask.

'Why did I leave? Because I thought that you were growing tired of me. That my own personal twelve months with you were coming to an end. That any minute you were going to tell me it was over.'

'Never! Oh, I may have kicked and struggled a bit—fought against admitting it until the very last minute, but only because I was terrified. I didn't know what was happening to me. I'd never felt that way before—never felt so vulnerable, so exposed, so defenceless. And when you seemed to change…'

'If I changed it was because I felt vulnerable too. Because I was scared of what was happening to me. And I didn't dare say it because I thought that you were determined on what we'd agreed on from the start—that no ties, no commitment sort of relationship.'

'And I'm to blame for that.' Joaquin's tone was wry. 'I insisted on that from the start and I never told you the way that my feelings were changing. I was too weak, too afraid to open myself up to you. But I should have told you. Told you that you're the woman that I adore. The woman who rocked my world, turned it and all my plans and schemes, my carefully thought-out path through life, right on their head. You had me thinking about weddings and rings and happily ever afters...'

Suddenly he lifted his hand, splaying long fingers out over the pit of her stomach where, she hoped so desperately now, perhaps the earliest beginnings of a new life were starting to grow.

'And children,' he said softly, almost reverentially. 'So, my darling Cassandra, my love, my heart, my life, if I were to ask you again...'

But Cassie couldn't wait. She didn't need to wait to hear the words. She knew her answer, and she was impatient to get it out and let him know once and for all time that she was his and only his.

'Joaquin Alcolar,' she said with mock severity, 'you really are making a meal of this. Are you trying to ask me to marry you yet again?'

'That's exactly what I'm trying to do,' Joaquin told her sombrely. 'And I'm trying my damnedest to get it right this time.'

'Oh, Joaquin!'

It was a sigh of pure bliss, of total, perfect happiness, and her joy shone in her face, making her eyes gleam like the most brilliant sapphires in all the world.

'You've got it right, my darling, believe me—you couldn't get it more right if you tried.'

Reaching down, she caught hold of his hand and pulled him towards her, lifting him off his knees and into her arms, holding him as close as she possibly could.

'And the answer's yes, my love. Yes, yes, yes! So now will you please hurry up and kiss me before I die of impatience?'

Joaquin's smile matched hers for brilliance as he looked down into her lovely face, and his jet eyes gleamed softly with the deep inner glow of the love that he felt in his heart.

'Nothing would give me more pleasure,' he assured her and bent his head to prove just that.

Introducing a brand-new miniseries

For Love or Money

This is romance on the red carpet...

For Love or Money is the ultimate reading experience
for the reader who has a taste for tales of wealth and
celebrity and the accompanying gossip and scandal!

**Look out for the special covers
on these upcoming titles:**

Coming in September:

EXPOSED: THE SHEIKH'S MISTRESS
by Sharon Kendrick #2488

As the respected ruler of a desert kingdom, Sheikh Hashim
Al Aswad must marry a suitable bride of impeccable virtue.
He previously left Sienna Baker when her past was exposed—
he saw the photos to prove it! But what is the truth behind
Sienna's scandal? And with passion between them this hot
will he be able to walk away...?

Coming soon:

HIS ONE-NIGHT MISTRESS
by Sandra Marton #2494

SALE OR RETURN BRIDE
by Sarah Morgan #2500

HARLEQUIN®
Presents

Seduction and Passion Guaranteed!

www.eHarlequin.com

HPTSM

If you enjoyed what you just read,
then we've got an offer you can't resist!

Take 2 bestselling love stories FREE!

Plus get a FREE surprise gift!

WIVES *Wanted!*

When a wealthy man wants a wife,
he doesn't always follow the rules!

Welcome to

Miranda Lee's

stunning, sexy new trilogy.

Meet Richard, Reece and Mike, three Sydney
millionaires with a mission—they all want to get
married…but none wants to fall in love!

Coming in August 2005:

BOUGHT: ONE BRIDE #2483

Richard's story: His money can buy him anything
he wants…and he wants a wife!

Coming in September:

THE TYCOON'S TROPHY WIFE #2489

Reece's story: She was everything he wanted in a wife…
until he fell in love with her!

Coming in October:

A SCANDALOUS MARRIAGE #2496

Mike's story: He married her for money—
her beauty was a bonus!

HARLEQUIN®
Presents

Seduction and Passion Guaranteed!

www.eHarlequin.com

HPWW

Coming Next Month

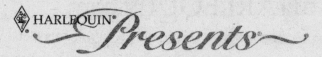

HARLEQUIN *Presents*

THE BEST HAS JUST GOTTEN BETTER!

#2493 THE BRAZILIAN'S BLACKMAILED BRIDE Michelle Reid
The Ramirez Brides
Anton Luis Scott-Lee is going to marry Cristina Marques. She rejected him years ago and his payback will be sweet: she will be at Luis's bidding—bought and paid for! But Luis will find that his bride can't or *won't* fulfill all of her wedding vows....

#2494 HIS ONE-NIGHT MISTRESS Sandra Field
For Love or Money
Lia knew that billionaire businessman Seth could destroy her glittering career. But he was so attractive that she succumbed to him—for one night! Eight years on, Lia's successful. When he sees Lia in the papers, Seth finds that he has a love child, and is determined to get her back!

#2495 EXPECTING THE PLAYBOY'S HEIR Penny Jordan
Jet-Set Wives
American billionaire Silas Carter has no plans for love—he wants a practical marriage. So he only proposes to beautiful Julia Fellowes as a ruse to get rid of her lecherous boss and to indulge in a hot affair—or that's what he lets her think!

#2496 A SCANDALOUS MARRIAGE Miranda Lee
Wives Wanted
Sydney entrepreneur Mike Stone has a month to get married—or he'll lose a business deal worth billions. Natalie Fairlane, owner of the *Wives Wanted* introduction agency, is appalled by his proposition! But the exorbitant fee Mike is offering for a temporary wife is *very* tempting...!

#2497 THE GREEK'S ULTIMATE REVENGE Julia James
The Greek Tycoons
Greek tycoon Nikos Kyriades wants revenge—and he's planned it. He'll treat Janine Fareham to a spectacular seduction, and he has two weeks on a sunny Greek island to do it. If Janine discovers she's a pawn in his game, Nikos knows she'll leave—but it's a risk he'll take to have her in his bed!

#2498 THE SPANIARD'S INCONVENIENT WIFE Kate Walker
The Alcolar Family
Ramon Dario desperately wants the Medrano company—but there is a condition: he must marry the notorious Estrella Medrano! Ramon will not be forced into marriage, but when he sees the gorgeous Estrella, he starts to change his mind....

HPCNM0905